D1479295

Wedding Bells
in
Beacon

TERRY GARRETT

Wedding Bells in Beacon
© 2022 Terry Garrett

Paperback ISBN: 978-1-66783-404-7
eBook ISBN: 978-1-66783-405-4

Dedicated to my daughters Ali and Kate.
In loving memory of my son Jason.

Chapter 1

MAGGIE MISSED JACK WITH A VENGEANCE, yet she understood why he had to go. His colleague from the old practice in Chicago asked him to be a member of the team going to Haiti for a stint with Doctors Without Borders. They were needed to deal with the after effects of a 6.9 magnitude earthquake near Port-au-Prince. Hundreds of lives were lost, but they could help the injured. With Jack's big heart and his innate need to be of service, he, of course, went. He left on April 1 and it had only been a week, but it felt like much longer to her.

Before leaving he asked Maggie if she would consider moving out to the country house, the home he had purchased early in January. Since moving to Beacon, Jack had been temporarily living in an apartment and when the stone lodge on the pond just a couple of miles from town became available, he knew he had found his home. Maggie loved it too; she was also crazy about her old craftsman but would give it up for the new life they were building together once they were married. She was old-fashioned, she supposed, but she wanted to make it official and although she wasn't the kind of decorator that wanted to flip homes, she did love turning a house into a home and had done just that over the years with her place. She also desired the familiar feel of her own surroundings while Jack was away so she chose to remain there and to keep to her usual routine.

She doesn't feel brushed aside this time, only proud of the man she loves. When her ex-husband left her 14 years ago to begin a new life with a younger woman, she felt very differently— very alone and all of a sudden, not good enough. It had taken her years to recapture her confidence, but together she and her daughter Kate had somehow made it through the tough transition.

Over the years she had gradually grown into a stronger, more independent woman than she was when she had been married and subsequently dumped, and was ready to be an equal partner in a new relationship. Now in her 50s, she supposed one of the benefits of aging is the wisdom gained. And that, along with the most amazing man unexpectedly dropping into her life was a gift to treasure.

Maggie rinsed out her coffee cup, cleaned out the french press and switched off the kitchen light. She glanced at her watch and realized it was time to head to the yoga studio she owned with Kate. Pausing at the old oak mirror in the front hallway, she ran her fingers through her short hair to give it a little style, applied some light coral lipstick, and pushed up the sleeves of her gray yoga top. Maggie had a noon class to teach. The studio was just a few blocks away in the lovely Beacon village, and it was a perfect spring day. She decided to walk. Maggie didn't even need to throw on a sweater. The sun was shining brightly overhead in the crystal blue Carolina sky, so she slipped into her most comfortable leather loafers and made her way outside. Standing on the front porch, she took a moment to just drink in the beautiful day. The warm breeze caressed her face, and the honeysuckle and jasmine vines covering the nearby picket fence wafted their mingled fragrances her way.

As Maggie reached the downtown corner, she noted the progress that Kate and her fiance Dan were making on the B&B he purchased just before Christmas. She hoped they would accomplish their goal of being opened by the first of June. Things looked promising. The biggest change she could see was the spacious lawn starting to take shape. So much of the dense overgrowth had been cleared to reveal what a lovely yard it could be. She gazed with appreciation at the seating area just off the side porch where guests would soon sit comfortably in the shade of an oak tree easily over 200 years old. She visualized visitors enjoying an iced tea or glass of wine after browsing the charming shops in the Beacon village, just steps away. The house itself was also in bad shape when Dan bought it, but a new coat of white paint and forest green shutters have brought it back to the way it looked in early pictures depicting the first stately homes in Beacon.

Todd Tadlock's company truck was on site--Tadlock Home Renovations emblazoned on the side panel. He lived in nearby Charlotte, but was here working on the future B&B for a couple of months. Getting out of his truck, he waved to Maggie as she walked by. She had to admit he was handsome, probably close to her age, tall with sandy blond hair and a short beard. She could see his muscular build through his tight t-shirt and close fitting blue jeans. His looks were appealing, but there was something about the man that she didn't trust. Well, she was glad to see the improvements he was making anyway. That was what mattered, after all.

Turning the corner, she felt herself smiling as she peered inside the Ivy Cafe, now flourishing. Dan had opened it only four months ago. Almost lunch time, customers were seated and enjoying a late breakfast or early noon meal. Just next door she reached the yoga studio and felt the happiness and gratitude she always did when entering the business that she and her daughter had built from scratch.

"Hi Kate," she greeted her daughter who was manning (shouldn't the word be "womanning"?) the front desk.

"Hey Mom!" Kate was glad to see her. She was ready to get on with her to-do list and get outside on this gorgeous day. "Looks like your class is full this noon. Have a good one." She gave her mom a quick hug, gathered up her iPad and her faithful companion Freddie. "See you later. We are headed to the B&B to check on today's progress." Kate looked fit in her heather gray leggings and snug fitting white yoga top. Stepping into her favorite leopard print tennis shoes, she brushed a stray strand of hair from her face. "Can't wait to get outside and breathe in this day." She wrote a quick text to Dan, knowing he was knee-deep in the kitchen next door and walked the half block to the B&B, which would also soon be her home.

Maggie waved goodbye and prepared to teach the noon class. She couldn't help but reminisce about Jack arriving in town, taking Kate's class, then the two of them spotting him at Riggio's back in November. It had actually been the night before Thanksgiving. She had tried to look disinterested, but Kate caught on right away that she was drawn to him. Then when Kate hurt herself and they had rushed to the clinic the very next day, she was pretty delighted to meet the new doctor in town and realize that she already knew him, at least by sight.

Chapter 2

ONCE THROUGH THE GATES AT THE FUTURE INN, Freddie was happy to break loose and run around the property. All the construction crew knew to leave the gate securely latched so he could roam free; a vizsla needed to run off extra energy, especially after a long morning of serving as ambassador at the yoga studio. Kate poured a tall glass of lemonade and went out onto the porch to relish the feel of the warm midday sun on her back. If she just had the whole afternoon, she thought, she could sit here all day. However she knew she only had a few minutes to spare; there wasn't time for a book and a porch swing this afternoon. Reluctantly, she stepped inside. Aah. The sound of a screen door slamming meant springtime had arrived in earnest.

Dan had purchased the rundown house when it came up for sale in December, knowing how much Kate had always admired the grand old Wilson place back when they were kids, and thinking what a great location it promised for him, not only to live, but also to provide a B&B around the corner from his cafe. In severe disrepair, the century-and-a-half old home was in need of plenty of renovation before he could open, he hoped by summer. He was not in a position to realistically fund all that needed doing, but being financially backed by Maggie's new boyfriend, Jack, made all the difference, and he was able to hire Todd Tadlock's company to help make the dream come true.

Kate stepped carefully into the kitchen, one of the rooms that had to be almost gutted to accommodate the cooking that would go into serving guests. She found Tadlock in there supervising a couple of guys and discussing the layout they would use to install new shelving and cabinets. She felt him eyeing her slowly from top to bottom before she even saw it. Greeting him with a curt nod, she left him to his work, and as she went into the dining room, she couldn't shake the uncomfortable feelings she had whenever she was around him. Creepy was too strong a word, but maybe slick was the right moniker. She was especially wary of the completely unwanted attention he was paying to her mom.

She quickly exited and went upstairs to check the progress on their future bedroom and en-suite before leaving to walk over to her bungalow, so she could catch up on some of her own household chores. As she and Freddie ambled toward home, Kate started dreaming of the wedding they would have in the yard of the B&B, the sooner the better. She was head over heels in love with Dan. Always had been.

Dan was busy, as usual, at the cafe around 1 p.m. and was happy to have received Kate's text more than an hour earlier. Finally, the two of them were back together where they had always been meant to be. He shook his head and shuddered as the thought passed through his mind that he could have lost her. He had been such a fool to stay away for so long. And on the work front, his passion for cooking was fulfilled every day. He had been able to hire a couple of great employees. Josh, especially, was turning out to be a godsend. And more and more customers were returning fairly regularly. He just knew in his heart the cafe would become an integral part of life in Beacon and the village shopping area.

The B&B was also closer each day to becoming a reality. Somehow, he would find the energy and the time to accomplish it all. Kate had wondered if he could manage both, and he had assured her that he liked keeping busy. But this was beyond busy. They didn't have much time together right now.

His spring menu had just debuted and his regulars seemed to be ready to dig into the new recipes. He personally thought of spring as "asparagus season". His grilled asparagus with parmesan was the most popular side dish on the menu. The entire menu was lighter fare but still comfort food enough to please. He felt like he had finally found his niche.

"Hey Dan," he was greeted by Todd Tadlock as he momentarily stepped around front to the cafe counter. "How's it going?" his contractor asked as he looked up at the chalkboard menu determining what he wanted to order.

"Going well Todd, thanks," Dan replied. He observed, just before Todd placed his order, that his future mother-in-law was just now coming in for lunch as well. Maggie approached the counter, stood behind Todd, and ordered her usual, using sign language understood by Dan and herself. She sat down at a small table.

Todd placed his order for a reuben and the soup of the day and sauntered over to Maggie. The place was almost full and he was glad. He wanted an excuse to sit with her. "Hi Maggie, you look fine as usual; say, do you mind if I share your table? The place is crowded today." He smiled broadly and began to take a seat at her table before she could respond.

"Sure I guess, uh," Maggie mumbled her response. He was a nice enough guy she supposed, but she would have preferred being alone for lunch today. She found her manners, "How is it going over at the B&B?" she inquired politely. Somehow she just felt a little uncomfortable around him. He hadn't overstepped or anything like that, but he just seemed, uh, maybe interested in more than she would ever want in a friendship. She pushed away the thought. She was probably just letting her imagination run wild.

"It's a big project as I'm sure you have figured out already, but I like the work," he replied. "The transformation will be bigger than anything I have ever done before. I'm up to the task. It's a nice challenge."

"Do you think it can be ready by early June for their opening?"

" I do," he told her. "I think that it could be anyway, but unforeseen complications always seem to come up in this line of work."

They were interrupted when Dan stopped over at their table. He asked his remodeling expert what they were working on today, and Todd responded that they were finalizing kitchen decisions. Dan was pleased to hear that because cooking all his meals at the cafe was getting to be a little monotonous, not to mention inconvenient. As the two men talked shop, Maggie took advantage of the opportunity to get up and say her goodbyes.

A few minutes later when Todd opened the door to exit the cafe, he looked around for Maggie. He was disappointed that she wasn't still on the sidewalk out front. He knew she was trying to tell him that she was in some kind of a relationship with a doctor, but heck, the doc wasn't around and Todd was. He figured she was fair game. A strong magnetic pull was attracting him to her. She wasn't like any woman he knew and she certainly was more interesting than Tiffany, a woman in Charlotte that he was seeing off and on. Sure, Tiffany was built. But Maggie was classy.

DAN FINISHED WORKING AT THE CAFE a couple of hours later and went home to check on the day's progress. Walking the half-block from the cafe to the B&B, he smiled as he thought about his daily commute. A lot different than it had been in New York City. Man, he was glad that life was in the rearview mirror. Relationships were so much easier in Beacon. People were genuine and he realized that he was starting to build a team at the cafe that he could count on. Take Josh, for example. He had really lucked out when that young man had come in over the Christmas season looking for work for the Spring. Having just graduated early from college at midterm, he needed a job until he hoped to find a teaching job by fall. Dan didn't know what he would have done without him.

Once home, he entered through the side door, stroked Freddy's fur, then went up the back stairway to what would soon be Kate's and his master bath. The old bedroom at the top of the stairs had been the servants' quarters decades ago and was such a dark depressing space. The new room would be filled with light and opened up into a bath and closet space. Just off the other side of the bedroom he was anticipating morning coffee with Kate as they would be able to walk onto their small balcony and greet each day. Together.

His cell rang and he almost disregarded it. So often the calls he didn't recognize were spam, but he saw his buddy Brooks's number. Wondering why he would be calling midday, Dan answered, "Hey Brooks, how's it going?" Brooks and Reese were high school friends of his and Kate's, but years ago, they had moved to the Virginia coast. The two men had stayed in touch by calling each other every New Year's Eve, pretty regular as far as guys were concerned.

"Not going so well," Brooks told him and Dan could hear the defeat in his voice. "That's why I'm calling. Our place was severely damaged by the storm over the weekend. It looks like we need somewhere to go for a few weeks at least while repairs are being made."

"Man, I'm sorry to hear that, but you might have called the right guy. Is Reese okay with coming back? I know y'all moved away so you could start somewhere new after the accident. I mean, hey, we would love to have you here, but, well you two must have already talked about that, huh, or you wouldn't be asking. Kate and I are rehabbing an old place. Remember the Wilson house on the corner by the village? I bought it and we are turning it into an inn, a B&B. It's still pretty rough so if you don't have high expectations and are willing to rough it, live with construction noise…"

"I'd heard about that Dan, and no pressure, but I had an idea about the house and wanted to run it by you. Reese doesn't even know I'm calling. I didn't want to get her hopes up. She's pretty down about the wreckage at our place. I'm sure you can imagine." Dan heard him sigh. "I guess I had better make sure she'd be alright. Her memories of Beacon are still great ones; she had a happy childhood. I may be being insensitive to her though. I'd better find out. She and I weren't ready to move back there after college. She wasn't ready, but I think she'd be good with it now. I'll talk to her."

"What were you thinking about coming back?" Dan asked.

"Well, I, uh, I wondered if you might have room for us, given that, in exchange I would help you work on the place. And Reese loves to decorate. Maybe she could be of help as well. No big deal if it won't work for you though."

"Wow, I think it might be just what we need. We'd love to have you two here, and I think it could be a win for both of us. Let me run it by Kate." Dan thought about how nice it would be to have some help. He hadn't told Kate how overwhelmed he felt about everything , but he had the sense she was starting to notice.

" Of course, and no worries if it won't work for y'all. Hey, man, it might not even work for Reese. I'll see what she thinks about it."

"Talk soon," Dan replied.

That evening Dan discussed Brooks's and Reese's dilemma with Kate. She didn't hesitate for a moment.

"Sure," she said, "invite them to come. The more the merrier, but do you think Reese will want to come?"

*   *   *

RECIPES

Asparagus with parmesan

Preheat oven to 400 degrees. Wash asparagus and snap off the bottom ends. In a bowl, mix olive oil. salt and pepper to taste. Pour onto parchment covered sheet pan. Roast about 15 to 20 minutes and remove from oven. Generously sprinkle on Parmesan while hot.

Reuben. Makes 1.

- 2 slices of best cinnamon raisin bread you can find

- Softened butter

- Good thousand island dressing

- Two slices Swiss cheese

- 1/4 lb corned beef

- 1/4 cup sauerkraut, extra juice squeezed out.

Make it like you would a grilled cheese. Still good if you omit the beef for vegetarians.

Chapter 3

KATE AND DAN STAYED UP LATE THAT NIGHT, excited about the possibility of having Brooks and Reese back, even for a little while, but wondering if it could really happen or if their friends would decide the memories would be too painful. They had all been good friends in high school. Brooks had been a forward on the basketball team with Dan and Chris. He was a handsome kid with great Italian looks, but they sure felt sorry for Brooks Carpenter at times, living with his grandma and being so responsible for her, especially with so little money to live on.

Life had dealt him a tough hand, but Brooks had never complained, and he was a standout at basketball, winning him a full ride at UNC. He could have won an academic scholarship as well. He was a whiz at math and now worked as an accountant. He and Reese O'Donnell Greenland had fallen for each other their senior year of high school. They could not have come from more different backgrounds. He'd been born to teenage parents and raised by his maternal grandma. Her dad was a prominent attorney in Beacon, and her mom opened Greenland's clothing store on South Main when they were all still little kids. Reese always loved to read and that wasn't any surprise to anyone. Her parents were the biggest patrons of the library of anyone in town. Reese was fair, Irish, smart, always reading something, and as genuinely nice as they come.

She and Brooks had known each other all their lives but didn't grow close until they sat next to each other in homeroom their senior year. They talked every morning that year and soon became an inseparable couple. She went to UNC with him and they grew even closer in college. Reese's dad had a small airplane. He and her mom flew to all of Brooks's games. They usually took his grandma with them. She was aboard the plane when they ran into unexpected bad weather on the way home from an away game at Florida State. The plane went down in the woods not far from Tallahassee and all three lives were lost. The entire town of Beacon had been devastated, and of course, Reese's and Brooks's lives were changed forever. Kate and Dan relived that memory and neither of them slept well after talking about it that night.

MAGGIE'S SISTER ALI HAD A PHONE CALL FROM AN OLD FRIEND HERSELF THAT WEEK. Her roommate from college, Stacy Tolle, had pursued a career as a visiting nurse. Stacy was a kind-hearted woman who seemed to have wanderlust wired into her core being. The visiting nurse's life has been a perfect match, combining her desire to care for others and her itchiness to never stay in one place for long. Gregarious by nature, no matter where she went she never knew a stranger.

Now her career was bringing her to Charlotte for a position at a nursing home and she needed a temporary place to stay while she looked for something a little more permanent. Ali wished she could invite her to move in with them, but with the four boys, their house was stretched to the limits already. She told Stacy she would help her find a place.

Later that week Ali was out shopping with Kate and Maggie for Kate's wedding dress and casually remarked that Stacy needed a place to stay temporarily. Kate overheard from the dressing room and mused out loud about Dan's dad's place. Harold was in London and the huge home was empty. Maybe Stacy could stay there and serve as a caretaker at the same time. Ali thought that might be a plan and said as much. Kate replied that she would check with Dan that night. He didn't relish conversations with his dad, but that one shouldn't cause any confrontation. Ever since Dan's mom died when he was only twelve, he had a strange, difficult relationship with his dad that had only worsened as time passed.

As Dan and Kate relaxed on the porch swing after dinner, she brought up the need for Stacy to find a temporary place to land. "Since the only extra bedroom we have ready will be occupied by Reese and Brooks, do you think it might work for her to stay at your dad's and serve as a caretaker? At least the house wouldn't be empty."

"Jeez, don't know he will respond but I don't mind calling dad about an idea like that. The most he can say is no. And I'm not sure he would since it's a win for him as well, having someone take care of the house. I'll call him tomorrow when the six hours time difference works for both of us." Dan's mind went back in time to when the difficult father he had growing up finally checked out of any shred of a relationship they might have had. He'd never been the kind of dad that spent time with him—no ball, no model airplanes, not much affection, and no rough house play. Then after his mom died…

Kate interrupted his thoughts. "I hope it works out." Over the years she had gotten to know the outgoing and loveable Stacy when she came to visit her Aunt Ali. She wanted the best for her. The two gazed up at Todd Tadlock as he got into his truck to leave for the day. "I wish he didn't give me the heebie-jeebies," Kate admitted.

"I know. I don't like the way he is around your mom either. But his work seems top notch."

BACK HOME IN HER KITCHEN Maggie was sipping a glass of Sauvignon Blanc while talking for a few minutes on FaceTime to Jack. She could see the weariness in his features and wanted to be able to hug some of the tired away. Instead, she managed a bright smile and asked how it was going. Jack told her, "Now that we are here and seeing patients all day long, I feel like we are making a difference. I wish I had more surgical ability, but I have enough to assist. It's so hard seeing people live like this in such disastrous conditions. And I miss you."

"I miss you so much," she responded, "I love you. I'll let you get some rest."

"I love you more." He looked exhausted to her.

Maggie closed her iPad and poured another small glass of wine, reflecting on the first time she talked to Jack at the yoga studio. He captured her attention when he smiled and his blue eyes sparkled as his face crinkled up in such an endearing way. That early impression was nice, but as their relationship deepened, what she grew to appreciate most was his big heart, open to her and a new life together. She couldn't have even dreamt him up in her imagination. Life hadn't been this complete for her in as long as she could remember. She wrapped herself up in a big hug. She wanted him safely back home.

EARLY THE NEXT MORNING Dan called his dad in London knowing it would be noon his time. "Son, make it quick," his dad greeted him in typical fashion. "I have a meeting in five minutes." Dan let out a sigh. "I just want to run something by you." He filled him in.

"How did it go?" Kate inquired .

"Typical Harold but at least he said yes."

"That's all we could hope for," she said. "I love you, got to run." With a quick hug and kiss she and Freddie were off to the yoga studio. On the short walk to the studio she thought about how much had changed over the past six months and all for the better, all except for how busy they were. But she was sure that it would improve. Soon, she hoped. This time a year ago she would not have imagined that Dan would be back in her life, or that they would be about to be married and living in the old Wilson Place, having turned it into a B&B. She was grateful that she hadn't dated anyone else too seriously, or worse, married someone else. Life was busy now, but that's what made it fun as well. Most of the time. Time for class. "Come on Freddie. Let's go in!"

They walked inside and Kate was greeted by the familiar welcoming fragrance of lemongrass oil. A couple of her early birds came in right behind her and she was happy as usual to see Norm Meade. He was a regular and Kate always enjoyed having him in the class. He and Barb started practicing there when she and her mom first opened almost ten years ago. About three years ago Norm's wife of twenty years was diagnosed with breast cancer. Their lives upended, Norm's and Barb's two daughters cared for her and pursued every opportunity for care but she lost her battle within that year.

Kate was impressed with his yoga practice. Norm was in his early fifties, stocky, fit, compactly built at no taller than 5 ft 5, strawberry curly blond haired and fair-skinned, his presence loomed larger than his height. She supposed it was because of his confidence, kindness, and dedicated yoga practice. He always placed his mat squarely in the middle of the room and that alone spoke volumes. He didn't need to be in the front row, but he wasn't timidly seeking to hide in a back corner either.

Norm lived in the same block as Dan's childhood home in one of the stately early Beacon houses. He drove a BMW convertible and seemed to have fairly flexible work hours doing something with the internet that Kate always assumed made him a good deal of income. She wondered if he had wanted to start dating again, always sensing a loneliness in him. Oh well, time for class. Enough musing about one of her students.

Later that morning she talked to her Aunt Ali about the good news that her friend Stacy could stay at Dan's dad's house. "Oh fantastic," Ali replied. "She'll be here by tomorrow and I didn't know what we were going to do to shuffle around beds. She will feel like a queen staying at that amazing home. And I think she will be good for the place too. Empty houses don't sit well alone."

"I'm excited to see her again. She was always such a bubbly and fun person to be around," Kate said.

"Well I would expect she will be at the yoga studio before you know it. She loves yoga!"

"That sounds great, love you, talk soon." Kate had to get on with a busy day and was set to meet her best friend Jenny for a cup of coffee in fifteen.

Dan and Kate were best friends throughout high school with Chris and Jenny Spring and their friendship had only continued to grow over the years. Jenny was a busy realtor, primarily selling commercial properties, so the two women usually squeezed coffee time between Kate's yoga classes and Jenny's real estate showings. Today Kate was eager to tell her about their old friends, Brooks and Reese, coming to stay after the storm damaged their home on the coast in Virginia.

The two friends hugged when they arrived outside the coffee shop at the same time, then went in to buy coffee and visit. Kate had always been close to Jenny, but, if possible, loved her even more after her part in making sure Kate and Dan got back together at Christmas time. Sitting in their favorite easy chairs in front of the window, Kate brought up the news about Brooks and Reese Carpenter coming back to stay for a bit.

"I'm sorry that happened to them, but I'm happy to hear they'll be here for a while. That's great news. It'll be fun to spend time with them again. It's been years!" Jenny was her usual upbeat self. She paused, drank a sip of coffee, reflecting on the tragedy that had taken Brooks's grandma and Reese's parents. "Are they okay coming back, though?"

"I think so. Dan had asked Brooks the same thing when he first called, and Brooks talked it over with Reese and they both felt ready. He also mentioned to Dan that they would be willing to help out getting the B&B ready to open. I don't even remember what they are doing for work now. Last I heard, Reese was working at a bookstore, I think."

"That's right. She has always been a voracious reader and Brooks works as an accountant, I'm pretty sure." Jenny changed the topic to Kate's wedding plans. "Are you any closer to setting a date for the wedding?"

"We want to have it in early June, or even better, late May so we don't conflict with opening the B&B in June, but I sometimes think we would be rushing it all too much to enjoy the planning."

"Well, have you thought about maybe having it be the first thing at the B&B, kind of a soft open, with your friends and family from out of town as your first guests?"

"That is an incredible idea. I think I'll share that thought with Dan." Kate was open to the possibility. She wondered why she hadn't thought of it. They talked a few more minutes then went their separate ways—Jenny to show a property, Kate to teach another class.

That evening after dinner Kate mentioned to Dan what Jenny had suggested about the wedding date. As they sat on the porch swing enjoying the comings and goings of the patrons at the brewery in the old fire station across the street, they both found themselves relaxing for the first time that day.

"Jenny's idea for our wedding was to have a sort of soft opening with friends and family staying here and our ceremony could be the weekend just before we open. I think it could work. How about you? Could we pull it off, especially if we keep it simple?"

"So," Dan responded, brushing a wisp of her hair that the April breeze was rearranging into her eyes. "We could go with maybe, let's see," he looked at the calendar on his phone… "Saturday, June 9th. That would give us an extra week before we host paying guests. I think I like it too. And simple sounds good to me."

Kate leaned her head on his shoulder. "And maybe we could open that next Wednesday instead of waiting for the weekend. How does that sound to you? Sunday through Tuesday we could iron out any problems that come up at the soft open."

"But that wouldn't leave us any time for a honeymoon." He squeezed her hand. "I don't want you to be disappointed."

She returned the squeeze. "Look, we can go somewhere later in the year. We need to get this place opened just right. We only have one chance to do it." She didn't want him to feel any more stress than he already did.

His reply was to wrap her up in a hug and a kiss to remind her how much he loved her.

Kate went inside to call her Aunt Ali about arranging for Stacy to stay at Dan's dad's house. "Hi, how are you Aunt Ali? Ready to get together for the key and the garage code for Stacy?"

"Sure Kate. I'm out walking with Declan and we can stop by the inn if you're home. I want to see the progress anyway."

"Sounds great. We will be out on the porch and ready with drinks for both of you. See you soon."

Ali and Declan arrived within the half hour, and Dan took them on a tour of the house. They sat on the porch afterwards, Ali sharing a bottle of Pinot Noir and providing Ali's son, Declan, with a frozen lemonade. Dan invited Ali to bring Maggie and Stacy to the Ivy Cafe for lunch tomorrow.

"Oh that would be fun, Dan," Kate added. "And it'll be our treat. Great idea!"

"I'm sure we can do that, see you then." Ali was relieved and excited. "Can't thank you two enough for what you are doing for Stacy." Declan thanked them for his lemonade, hugged his cousin, and high-fived Dan.

MEANWHILE, MAGGIE WAS AT HOME EAGER for her nightly call with Jack. She was a little disappointed when he didn't answer FaceTime. They'd only met each other six months ago, but her life had been immeasurably richer since meeting him and falling in love. Today she had made the mistake of googling Haiti and asking how safe it was there. The words jumped out at her: "There is nowhere safe in Haiti."

She wasn't a worrier by nature, but that got her going. She had meditated, prayed, and worried. All three. And it wasn't helping that he didn't answer. Oh, relief. He texted. 'Almost ready to operate. Can't talk but love and miss you. More than you can imagine.' Whew, it was enough. She could relax and go to sleep now.

Chapter 4

STACY'S ARRIVAL THE NEXT MORNING BROUGHT a new sense of excitement to their lives. She was that kind of spark plug. She bounced more than she walked, her smile lit up a room, and her brightness was more like sunshine than light bulbs. Not fussy about her appearance, she dressed casually in a tank top and cargo shorts, her shoulder-length brown hair was tossed up in a ponytail. Her natural beauty shone from within. Once Ali had her squared away at the Ivy household, they met Kate and Maggie at the cafe for lunch.

Stacy couldn't say enough about the cafe. She had been in Houston for her last assignment and the big city was fun. The Mexican food was without rival. But the charm of this quaint town was more to her liking. "I think I'm going to like it here," she told the women. "I already have three friends and that's three more than I had going into the last two places."

"Well," Ali told her old friend, "You will have several more in the near future if I know you; you've never known a stranger." She laughed and sat back to take it in that her good friend would be here for as long as this nursing job lasted, hopefully a good long while.

As they eagerly dug into their lunches, conversation flowed easily. So much to catch up on between Maggie's new relationship with Jack and Kate's whirlwind romance and big plans with Dan. Ali also had plenty to share about her brood of boys. Stacy was pretty excited as well about the yoga studio. She had joined a big busy studio in Houston and had been regular in attendance. A seasoned yogi, she could hardly wait to take a class from Maggie or Kate.

After lunch they went next door to give Stacy a tour of Beacon Yoga. She loved the look and feel of the studio. The exposed brick walls, early afternoon light spilling in through the large windows, and the smell of lemongrass was soothing, reminding her of the studio in Houston. She immediately decided to sign up for a first month of unlimited classes. One of the other teachers was working at the desk and introduced herself. "Hi, I'm Marie and I usually teach the yin classes. As a matter of fact, my monthly workshop is Saturday afternoon at four and some of us go out to a local Thai restaurant after. We'd love for you to join us."

Quick to join in the fun of a new experience, Stacy's big brown eyes grew bigger and she signed up for the workshop as well. She had learned that immersing herself into a new community as fast as possible was the best way to adjust to moving so often. "Well," Ali said admiringly, "you haven't changed a bit!" Ali and Stacy headed off to grab Stacy some moving-into-a-new-place necessities. Kate and Maggie stayed behind and sat in the office for a few minutes to discuss the wedding.

"Mom, great news! Dan and I set the wedding date for Saturday, June 9th. I had been talking over coffee with Jenny and she came up with the idea of us using it as a soft opening kind of weekend. So now the rush is on to get things finalized." Kate looked a little apprehensive as she told Maggie. Inside she was not confident about planning their wedding so quickly, but figured as long as they kept things simple and did first things first, checking off the to do list as they went, it would all go well.

"Oh Kate. That's exciting. And I think people today spend too much time planning anyway. Let's start a list and get going." Maggie had spent so much time and effort planning her own wedding down to the most minute detail; it sure hadn't made a difference in the long run. So much for that marriage. As far as Maggie was concerned, the wedding day itself took a backseat in importance to the relationship.

"Okay. I'm with you," Kate agreed and grabbed her laptop. "We already have started looking for my dress, and I guess we will get out there soon again. Then, I suppose invitations better go out since it's only a little over two months away." She felt a little panic at that thought, but kept the ideas flowing. "Roses will be in full bloom by then. And…"

"Kate, enough for now! My head is starting to spin." Maggie wasn't feeling as good about the short timeline the longer Kate made the list. "Talk to Dan about the invitations as soon as you can; everything will fall into place. It always works out." She sighed, deeply believing that to be true. Kate glanced down at her cell as the text notification beeped. "It's Reese. They will be here in about an hour. Where does the time go?" She gave her mom a quick hug and was on her way to the B&B.

She practically bumped into Dan as he walked out of the cafe next door at precisely the same moment. Laughing and giving him a quick kiss, Kate's mind flashed back to the day last November when she had run into him in the exact same spot. It had been years since she had seen him, and his showing up in Beacon had been a complete shock. So much had happened since then. And all for the good. "How did Stacy like your studio? Is she going to join?" he asked.

"Oh," Kate told him, "She is so in. She even signed up for Marie's workshop this Saturday. What an amazing woman! I admire the way she jumps into life. It doesn't surprise me that she is Aunt Ali's oldest friend."

"That's great! She'll make lots of friends that way."

"How are you managing to get away from the cafe so early?"

"Josh, the young guy I hired at Christmastime…you remember him? He graduated midterm from UNC Charlotte, Ruth from the bookstore's grandson? I hope I can keep him for a while. He's a hard worker and he's really great with the customers."

The two of them were already back at the B&B; Freddie jumped off the porch and ran to greet them at the iron gate. Being welcomed by her faithful canine was always a highlight of Kate's day. Dan turned to Kate, "I moved my stuff into one of the less finished bedrooms upstairs so Brooks and Reese can have the downstairs bed and bath. Not the greatest, so I hope they are comfortable enough." No sooner than the words were spoken, they saw their friends arrive and park out on the side street. Hugs and kisses all around, they welcomed them and ushered them into their house.

"Hey," Dan asked, "Everything's in the U-haul behind your car?"

"Yup, pretty much." Brooks and Reese had lost so much during the storm and pared down further, so that was it.

"Great. I have Kate's Aunt Ali's boys lined up to unload it. Her two oldest should be here in a few. Let's get it over to the side driveway closer to the house so they can get your stuff inside."

"Thanks, man. That's a great surprise. They don't mind?"

"They are great kids and they can always use the extra money."

"Well, we appreciate it. Moving is no fun. And dinner is on us." And since he knew Dan spent his days cooking, it was the least he could offer. He had heard that Riggio's was operating again, and they all loved that Italian restaurant. Brooks hadn't seen Julie and Mike since the fire and wanted to see how the rehab had gone.

"Deal, let us show you two around," Dan said.

"I can hardly believe the difference on the outside!" Reese exclaimed. "I remember the peeling paint, the shutters hanging off so loosely that it was a wonder they were still attached at all. Can't wait to get inside."

The place was still rough, but Kate and Dan were eager to show them the progress they had made, and afterwards, as Cheydon and Everett unloaded the trailer, the four old friends sat outside to enjoy the beautiful April day. The fragrant camellias and azaleas were bursting in bloom and it felt good to relax, even for a few minutes before heading to dinner.

They had decided to walk to Riggio's and were glad when Chris and Jenny could get a babysitter and join them spur of the moment. Once they were all seated, Julie Riggio stopped by their table to welcome them. Reese told Julie that they were sorry about the fire at Christmastime, but she marveled at the beautiful reconstruction. "I'm so glad you were able to restore the restaurant. It has always been our favorite," she told her. "We would like your house Chianti and some cheesy garlic bread for starters. Oh, and some calamari too, please."

"I'm glad you like the new look and feel of the place. We are really pleased. And your wine and appetizers will be coming right up," Julie promised and left to visit a nearby table.

As they munched on the appetizers and sipped the wine, Jenny asked Brooks and Reese what they were looking for as far as work was concerned. "Oh, I can work from the B&B for now," Brooks told her. "I'm an accountant, you probably remember, and I'm sure happy that the tax season is almost over. I'll be overloaded the next couple of weeks and then it should slow down and I can start helping with the B&B renovations."

Reese chimed in, "I worked at a bookstore in Virginia and really loved it. I have been thinking about opening my own store there." Reese had inherited a financial fortune when she lost her parents so money was definitely not an issue at all for her and Brooks. She had always hesitated to spend it, though, feeling deep down that not spending it was a way to honor her parents more. She was starting to realize now, though, that opening a bookstore was truly a way to honor them. They had both instilled a deep love of reading in her and had been so supportive of the Beacon library. Not spending her inheritance wasn't going to bring them back. She had to shake off the thought and reenter the present dinner conversation. Eight years had passed since the tragedy, but the waves of grief still reappeared to take her under without a moment's warning.

Chris jumped into the conversation. "Sounds great. Hope that works out well for you. Have to reach for those dreams." He glanced over at Dan and saw the weariness behind his eyes. Chris was Dan's oldest friend and could always tell when he was overwhelmed. He was starting to worry that Dan may have taken on more than even he could handle. He tried to push away the thought.

The rest of the dinner was like a mini reunion, with the six old friends catching up. Lots of shared memories, lots of laughter, lots of Chianti, and a few tears. As they walked home, Reese and Brooks admitted exhaustion and fell into their temporary bed, grateful to be there, even in the midst of all their belongings stacked around the room.

Chapter 5

THE NEXT AFTERNOON FOUND STACY excited to be walking over to the Beacon Yoga Studio for the yin yoga workshop. As she walked a few houses down from Dan's childhood home, she spotted another yogi toting his mat and water bottle as he secured his front door and soon joined her on the sidewalk, almost as if they had planned to meet there. That was all Stacy needed to take the opportunity to engage in conversation with the handsome stranger.

"Hi," she blurted out. "Going to the yin workshop?"

"I, um, am," he replied, looking at Stacy with wonder and a little confusion. "I don't believe I have ever seen you at the studio before." He might have had the beginning of a small smile on his face, but he looked pretty serious to her. She wondered what his story was. She returned his glance with that easy open smile of hers. Undaunted, she carried on, "Oh, I'm new here, but not new to yoga. Well, powerful flow yoga, but I have never taken a yin class, have you?"

"I practice there regularly. And, yes, I like vinyasa, but the yin is such a great complement to it. If there's a yin workshop and I can make it, I'm there." They walked and talked and before they knew it, they were at the studio. Marie welcomed them, a little surprised to see them come in together. Stacy noticed the perplexed look on her face and interjected, "We met as we walked over." She turned to look back at him, realizing they hadn't introduced themselves. "I'm Stacy, Stacy Tolle, by the way."

"Norm Meade," he extended his hand. He seemed a little shy, but Stacy didn't mind. She plopped her mat down next to his. Maggie was attending the workshop as well and her mat was just behind Stacy and Norm. She noticed they had met and wondered if they might eventually have a connection. "Stop it," she told herself to relax and focus on the yin.

After class, Marie invited all attendees to join them at the Thai restaurant to enjoy some time together. The usual gang showed up. Tammy, Eunice, Emma, Norm, Sue, Maggie, Johnny… and Stacy joined them. She had learned from all her moving around that jumping in feet first was the best way to immerse herself in a new community. No time like the present.

The conversation was stimulating. Marie brought up the subject that she'd had them meditate on while they held the long yin poses. She raised the topic of a coping mechanism we use to avoid feeling: to numb ourselves, and how healthy it can be to actually feel our feelings instead. So good to "go through them." Stacy had learned the hard way over the years to go through them, to feel them, kind of like walking through the night to get to the dawn. There really wasn't another way. Numbing oneself takes a toll eventually.

Afterwards as Maggie and Stacy walked to their respective homes together, Maggie filled Stacy in on her relationship with Jack–starting with her noticing him at Riggio's and then the pleasant surprise to find out that he was the new doctor at the clinic when Kate sprained her ankle on Thanksgiving Day. She filled her friend in on their history.

"I miss him so much that I can hardly believe it," she confessed. "And I'm worried about his safety in Haiti. Have you ever served there?"

"I haven't," Stacy shared, "but I have friends who have, and they've always come back safe and sound. I think they are cocooned in a protected environment as long as they don't stray from the medical site. Your man doesn't sound like a foolish guy. I hope that assures you a little anyway."

Maggie let out an audible sigh of relief. Just getting her fears out in the open with someone who had a listening heart had helped. Maggie was the first one to help anyone she could, but sometimes she kept her own worries bottled up. She felt so much better after opening up to Stacy. The two parted as they reached Dan's childhood home. "Sleep well," Maggie wished Stacy a restful night.

Maggie continued toward home and heard her phone ding, indicating a text. Quickly checking, hoping it was from Jack, she wasn't disappointed. His day had gone well, but he was off to bed, exhausted. She decided to send back a quick note to let him know how much she missed him and loved him. He needed the rest. She looked up to see a pickup truck slowing down; Todd Tadlock pulled over to offer her a ride. "No thanks, I'm almost home and it's a beautiful night," she refused politely.

"You sure?" he pressed.

"I'm sure." She smiled and waved him on his way, wondering what had kept him in town so late on a Saturday. He lived in Charlotte, after all. Oh, well, she dismissed the thought.

As she walked on it started to nag at her. What bothered her the absolute most was the memories he triggered of her ex-husband and his constantly roving eye, the lewd comments he made about other women right in front of her, the times she wondered if he was really working long hours. The day she found out that he wasn't. Tadlock reminded her of him. In a bad way.

BACK AT THE FUTURE INN, Dan was relaxing on the side porch, enjoying a beer with Brooks and discussing the remodel. "What can I do to help?" Brooks asked as he settled back in the lawn chair and grabbed a handful of barbecue potato chips.

"How about helping me work on the expanse of yard behind the house to get it cleared for the wedding? I know that you have an intense week left of tax prep, but whenever you have the time and energy."

"Consider it a plan." Brooks agreed. "It'll feel good to get outside after all the mental energy I expend on the taxes."

Dan grabbed another beer out of the cooler beside them. "That'll ease my mind. Thanks, man."

MEANWHILE, KATE AND REESE had gotten together with Jenny, Shanti, and Amy, all of them great friends in high school, and Reese was the only one who had moved away. Maybe it was the pinot grigio or maybe the beautiful backyard setting at Chris's and Jenny's, but Reese had to admit it felt amazing to be back with the gang again. She reminisced aloud, "Y'all are so fortunate to have remained close to each other. I mean, I feel close to all of you, but Virginia is a long way from here. We've made some new friends there, but you know what they say about old friends being the best friends." She sat back and sipped her wine.

"We love having you back, Reese, and although I don't want to wish you bad luck getting your house repaired, I for one would like for you to live here," Jenny blurted out. She was always quick to speak her mind.

"Oh," Kate added. "Let's play that game for a minute. I am going to have a house for sale really soon, and so is my mom! You have two opportunities right there," she winked at their realtor bestie as she made the suggestion.

Reese didn't stop them. She seemed to be all ears so Amy joined in with an idea of her own. "I heard through the grapevine that Ruth could use a little help over at Beacon Book Nook. I think that she is getting a little tired of the day to day and rumor is that she might want to spend more time with her grandkids." She hoped that she wasn't overstepping to bring it up. She didn't want to encourage Reese to move back for good if it would be too painful for her. She just wanted the old gang all back together again.

"All I have to add is an emphatic 'yes' to all of it!" Shantil chimed in. Reese had the goofiest smile on her face. Behind her smile was a very happy young woman thinking about everything they had just said. "I feel loved." She raised her glass to toast them all, "Here's to dreams coming true! Now, let's see what the universe has to say about that." She was feeling incredibly blessed, but even in those moments, she had the grief that had settled in to coexist with happiness. Somehow her heart had expanded to host happiness and sadness at the same time. She knew it was the same for Brooks. She had almost confided in her good friends about her desire to have a baby. Something kept it hidden inside her though, and she'd kept quiet.

Chapter 6

SUNDAY WAS GLORIOUS. Kate and Freddie walked over to the B&B in the morning. Since the cafe was closed on Sundays, she and Dan had planned to go there to eat breakfast and look at invitation designs, and hopefully finalize the guest list. Once he had pulled together some breakfast sandwiches, and she had filled a pot with coffee, they sat down at a corner table and started scanning the internet for ideas. Before long they were on a budget-friendly site and had found one with a picture of the bride and groom embracing in an outdoor environment. That looked ideal to them. They decided to go through some photos and find one of them with Freddie. That was going to be an easy item to check off the list. Maybe this wedding planning wasn't going to be such a challenge after all. Kate didn't want to add more to Dan's already overfilled plate. He poured each of them a cup of coffee. "What about flowers?"

"I was thinking, of course, we go with Tammy. She did such a fantastic job decorating the studio and cafe for the holiday festival Christmas Eve. Maybe she could cover an arch in front of the gazebo with roses. Since the yard will be beautiful in June, that may be all we need. Of course, we will want flowers at the reception afterwards too. Oh, no, where are we going to have that?"

"How about a big tent out in the yard? Plenty of room for the ceremony and the reception."

"I think that would be just right." Kate kissed him in agreement. "Let's go have some fun. Enough planning for today."

They gave Freddie the rest of the eggs, cleaned up, closed the cafe, and arm in arm in leash, headed out on the short walk back to the inn where they found Reese and Brooks, literally knee deep in the weeds clearing brush.

"Whoa guys! I said you could help out in the yard, but I didn't mean on Sunday morning!" Dan just shook his head at the sight of their friends working hard. He and Kate went inside to don work clothes and pitch in. After a couple of strenuous hours, progress was evident and they agreed to take a break on the porch to drink some iced tea and catch their breath.

Stacy wandered over about that time and burst through the gate, petting Freddie and laughing at the sight of the four young friends covered in dirt. "I just came by to let you know how much I appreciate my temporary digs," she managed to get the words out as soon as she could stop laughing. "I'm on my way to yoga and I am running a little early."

Kate offered her a seat on the porch. "Sit with us then for a few minutes if you'd like."

"Love to." Stacy took a seat, setting her yoga mat to the side. "I'm meeting Ali at the studio, but I was wondering about something, and since you are all from here..." They looked at her with curiosity. She went on, "I was wondering if you know Norm Meade."

"I grew up just down the street from him. Did you meet him on the block?" Dan asked her.

"I did. On the way to the yin workshop."

"Well, when I was young, he and his wife hung out with my parents. Their girls were much younger and I used to babysit while the adults went out. That was a long time ago. He's a nice guy," Reese recalled.

"So he's married?"

"No, sadly his wife passed away a couple of years ago. Cancer," Reese told her.

Stacy felt bereft at the news. "That had to be so hard." She glanced at her watch and sighed. "Probably better go meet Ali." They waved goodbye and sat back in their lawn chairs.

Kate said, "Wonder why she was asking, and she was either being polite or was distracted, not even mentioning how covered in dirt we all are."

"Well, when she got here she could hardly speak from all the laughing. I think she noticed," Dan looked down at his own clothes and shook his head.

STACY AND ALI ARRIVED AT THE STUDIO at the same time. Knowing her as well as she did, Ali was unnerved by Stacy's uncharacteristically quiet mood. "You okay?" she asked.

"Uh, yeah, I guess," Stacy tried to assure her, not very convincingly as far as Ali was concerned.

"Talk to me, " Ali requested, pretty firmly for her. She wasn't typically as upfront as Stacy. Hardly anyone was.

"Well, do you know Norm Meade very well?" She dipped a toe into the water.

Ali was about to respond when Norm entered the studio. The two women shared a quick glance, then turned to greet him.

Ali spoke, "Hi, you've met Stacy, Norm?"

"At the yin workshop yesterday, Yup. Shall we head in for class?" He opened the door. "Beauty before age," he ushered them in ahead of him. They all three rolled out their mats in the center of the room.

Maggie walked in to teach. She was covering class for one of the teachers who usually taught on Sunday mornings. She happily noted Ali's and Stacy's presence, then pushing her own agenda aside, she put on her professional hat and taught, focusing on every student in the class.

Once the class was over, Maggie noticed how Stacy's face was lighting up as she chatted with Norm. She couldn't be sure if it was just her imagination working overtime, but it looked like Norm might have a twinkle in his eyes as well. Maybe it was wishful thinking, but she wanted Norm to find happiness again and she could tell that Stacy was definitely interested in getting to know him better. Edging away, she started preparing the room for the noon class. Ali made her way towards Stacy as well, then saw the connection she and Norm were making. Quietly, she exited.

Chapter 7

SINCE TAX DEADLINE FELL ON A SUNDAY this year, Brooks had to work 24/7 for the next couple of days to wrap things up. After that he had assured Dan that he would be available any time to do anything he could to get the place ready both for the wedding and the opening. He had actually been looking forward to it since his day job took so much mental energy. Working in the yard felt great. When he was a little guy, his grandma had a big garden out in the backyard and he learned from an early age how to help out in the yard. Still, he was a bit surprised at how sore his muscles were after the exertion. It helped him to see that he needed more physical activity, and he told Reese as much, "Babe, I am sore from all that yardwork. I guess I need to spend more time doing stuff like that. I'm going soft."

Reese maneuvered her way around the suitcases that were still filling up their temporary bedroom to throw her arms around him. Gazing up at his big browns with her loving blue eyes, she assured him he was more than fine exactly as he was. And planted a big kiss on his lips to bring her point home.

"I liked digging in the dirt, babe, " Brooks suggested, "and after just a couple of days back with such good friends, it makes me wonder if we wouldn't like living in Beacon again." He knew he probably sounded a little crazy. After all, their life was in Virginia, not here. But what if? What if they could make the move? What was tying them to Virginia anyway? It felt right to be with old friends again.

Reese pondered his comments. After spending time with her girlfriends, she had been thinking maybe her idea about owning a bookshop would be better here. At least they would have support. She didn't bring it up to Brooks right then though. She did her best thinking inside her own head. He was more impulsive, which she had always found to be an interesting complement to the analytical accounting side of his personality.

The gals had told her that Ruth was thinking about retiring soon and the Beacon Book Nook could be for sale in the near future. Might not be a bad idea to go check it out one of these days. She had always loved spending time browsing the shelves and Ruth was so good at selecting just the right books. Oh, well, plenty to do just settling in here for the time being, she told herself.

Brooks interrupted her thoughts, "Well, I'm going to get back to work." Wrapping her up in a hug, he kissed her and turned to leave. He practically bumped into Kate as she was starting to knock on their door. Brooks laughed and greeted Kate, telling her he was heading off to work. Kate stepped in to check on Reese.

"How is it going?" she asked her.

"We are still living out of boxes, but I am so content being back here, happier than I had any idea that I would be, could be. Maybe, and I can't believe I'm saying this, but maybe it wasn't so bad that our house was messed up by the storm. I don't feel upset as much as I feel at peace. Crazy, huh?"

"I don't know. I kind of get it. And not to get too yoga-ey on you, but it makes me think of one of my favorite stories. Have you ever heard the old Chinese proverb about the farmer and his son?"

Reese shrugged her shoulders, "I don't think so."

"Well, the gist of it is…It was about 2,000 years ago. A farmer's horse runs away. His neighbor tells him that is bad news. The farmer says, 'Maybe. Maybe not.' The horse returns with another horse. Seems like good news, but the farmer's son rides the second horse, falls off, and breaks his leg. The farmer's neighbor tells the farmer that's bad news. The farmer replies that maybe it is, maybe it's not. About a week later the emperor comes and takes every able-bodied young man to fight in a war. The farmer's son is injured and is therefore spared. Good news. So basically, who's to say when something seems like bad luck, maybe it's not?"

"That's a cool story and it brings great perspective."

Reese sighed. After all, she was way too familiar with really bad luck. Sometimes she could couch what happened in hope, sometimes she couldn't.

"I think about it a lot," Kate returned. "Look what a turn my life took with Dan coming back home. Anyway, I don't mean to be pushy, but I was thinking about our talk the other night. Would you be at least interested in seeing my place, no pressure but—"

"Yes! Let's go," Reese surprised her. The two of them walked the few short blocks over to Kate's bungalow. Reese couldn't help but notice what a beautiful day it was. She loved the spring in Beacon: the early blooms, the green grass, the kids out biking, shooting hoops, the friendly neighbors waving their greetings …They reached Kate's house and Reese just stopped in her tracks, her mouth open, no words making their way out. Kate couldn't stand the anticipation. "Well, thoughts?"

"It's like a storybook cottage. I just, just love it. Can we go inside?"

They walked in and it was like watching an excited house hunter on HGTV. Every time they entered a new room, Reese expressed her love of the home that Kate had created over the past few years.

"How can you bear to sell it?" she asked.

"I am only handling it because of the home I will get to share with Dan. There's no other way I could, " she confessed. "Believe it or not, the hardest thing for me will be leaving my clawfoot tub. It's been my nightly ritual for so long."

"I get that, and I have to say I want Brooks to see this house, sooner the better."

"Sounds good to me, but remember, no worries if you don't decide to buy it, or even more, if you decide to stay in Virginia. I don't want to push you at all. Hey, want to head over to the bookstore and say hi to Ruth?"

They climbed up the steep, worn stairs onto the old wooden bridge that allowed pedestrians to cross over the railroad tracks. Everyone who visited Beacon seemed to enjoy the antique footbridge. It was hard to imagine but the narrow old structure was said to have carried cars in the early days. Once they had crossed the bridge, the bookstore was only a block down the street. They found Ruth busy helping a child select a new picture book for his little sister's birthday. Reese took a deep breath, inhaling the familiar scent of new books. She felt so at home there. Once Ruth finished helping the little one, she turned to see Reese and Kate.

"Will you just look at who the cat dragged in!" Her face lit up.

"Oh, Ruth!" Reese hugged her old friend. "I have missed you and this wonderful store." She wandered over to the romance section to see if there were any new novels in her favorite genre. Kate took the opportunity to pull Ruth aside and quietly ask her if the rumors were true about her possibly retiring.

"Oh, you've heard, have you?" She smiled wistfully. "I guess the grapevine in this small town is still going strong. Truth be told, I am thinking about it, but it is really important to me that if I sell, the Book Nook stays the Book Nook and doesn't get changed to some other kind of store. So I don't know," she mused, "but I appreciate your asking me instead of gossiping." Ruth still looked young to Kate; she must have found the fountain of youth playing with her grandkids and staying involved in community matters. The petite woman standing before her in dark jeans, white tee, and fitted black blazer, long gray hair pulled back in a ponytail, looked ten or more years younger than her seventy-five years.

"Of course," Kate replied and made her way over to see what Reese had found to read. Reese had a stack piled up and suggested that they check out before she bought out the section.

On the way home they talked about the possibility of Reese and Brooks purchasing the store if it did come up for sale. Reese's head was spinning with visions of moving back, buying Kate's house, owning a bookstore in their beloved Beacon, maybe having a baby…she could hardly wait to talk to Brooks. Could all this really happen?

As they neared the B&B, Kate spotted her mom and Aunt Ali sitting on the porch swing while drinking champagne! What? On a Sunday afternoon? Oh, my goodness! She raced up the sidewalk to see what possibly could have prompted them. Maggie's eyes lit up and Kate knew something was going on.

"Champagne, you two? Seems like a special occasion–"

"Oh, Kate, Reese! You won't believe it! Jack is coming home from Haiti tomorrow." She was gleeful.

Chapter 8

HOW EXCITING KATE THOUGHT, lingering in bed longer than usual and remembering yesterday's great news about Jack's return from Haiti. Her mom was so in love with him. Absence had definitely made her heart grow fonder in this case. He had only been away a couple of weeks, but when love is real, it is real. In her mom's case, it was so well deserved. It had dawned on her that there needed to be a celebration.

Maggie was all set to pick up Jack from the Charlotte airport at 5 p.m. so even with rush hour traffic they should be back by no later than 6:30. Kate had asked Dan last night if they could throw an impromptu welcome home at the cafe since it closed mid afternoon. He agreed that they could definitely pull that off.

Getting out of bed, she called her Aunt Ali to take care of the invites. Ali was slated to call her mom's old friend Dee and her husband, Stacy and Norm (there was something happening between them), Tammy, Mike and Julie Riggio, the staff at the clinic, and the teachers at the yoga studio, Jack's daughters and their families.

Dan was creating a simple tapas menu with Aioli on toasted sour-dough, homemade guacamole with lime tortilla chips, roasted asparagus with parmesan, Kate's favorite of hot pepper jelly over cream cheese with sesame crackers, fresh veggies, plenty of champagne, and desserts from the local bakery. Simple, but fun. Ali's boys were designing a homemade banner to hang across the front of the cafe so Jack could see it when they rounded the corner.

All Kate had told Maggie was that she and Dan wanted her to stop by the cafe so that they could welcome Jack home with a special dinner. Lots to do and yoga classes to teach, hers and her mom's, but luckily she had learned that slowly and surely there was enough time for everything. She just needed to focus on one task at a time. Envisioning her mom's and Jack's excitement fueled her with energy sufficient for the day.

IN THE MEANTIME, Reese and Brooks were taking an early morning stroll through the streets of Beacon, Reese gently guiding their walk to go past Kate's house, and if Brooks was up for it, to go inside and take a look. If that went well she thought they could meander by the bookstore and grab some coffee and chocolate croissants next door to sit down and talk about the possibility of moving back. Why not? They were young, mobile, and as the saying goes–if not now, when? She found it almost impossible to stifle her enthusiasm. She felt so alive.

Brooks took her hand as they walked down Providence on the sunny spring morning, the breeze gently rippling through their hair, the sun warming their backs, passing by the beautiful homes with early springtime flowers already bursting through the earth. The morning promised a glorious opportunity. Reese took a deep breath and squeezed her husband's hand. "This is Kate's home and she's going to sell it, obviously. She showed it to me yesterday and I have to say I kind of fell in love with it. Want to go inside?"

"Why not?" he returned her smile.

As they walked the brick path toward the porch, Brooks couldn't help but like the welcoming feel of the home, complete with the ubiquitous front porch swing. Stepping inside the inviting living room, he stopped. And stared. And found himself speechless. Finding his words, he turned to Reese, "I, I, er, it feels like home here. Let's look around." His initial feeling grew when he saw the bedrooms, and he couldn't help but visualize a nursery. As they stepped into the upstairs bathroom, he took in the shower and clawfoot tub and had to confess, "Reese, I do feel like this is us, but I wonder if we are jumping back into Beacon too fast. We just got here and this is supposed to be a way station on our way back to Virginia."

"I know," Reese admitted, "but I just feel so emotionally attached to our friends and Beacon again. And...I just want to make one more stop."

"Where?"

"Book Nook."

"Whoa."

"Just thinking about it, okay?"

"Let's go." He'd always had a hard time turning her down.

Hand in hand, they walked back to Main Street, across the railroad bridge, and down the street to the bookstore. As they stood outside the yet unopened shop that Monday morning, Reese told her husband about the conversation that Ruth and Kate had. "I think she is about to retire, babe," she told Brooks with exhilaration and apprehension both in her breathy, hopeful comment. "It would be a dream come true for me to own a bookstore here. I was thinking that you could set up shop in the back space for your accounting business —"

Brooks peered into the window and pressed his forehead against the pane. "Let's go into the coffee shop and talk."

MAGGIE WENT TO THE YOGA STUDIO and threw a load of lemongrass washcloths into the wash, sent out an email blast to their students regarding an upcoming special rate for new summer students, caught up on some paperwork, and left to go out and spiff up Jack's home. She wanted everything about his homecoming to be perfect.

Leaving the studio to drive the two short miles out of town, she ran into Todd Tadlock as he was parking his truck to eat an early breakfast at the Ivy Cafe. He invited her to join him for a bite, but she felt uneasy with him and hesitated. "I have a busy day. Jack is coming back from Haiti and I need to get his place cleaned up before he gets home."

"Well, I have a couple of free hours before the crew gets to the B&B. Why don't I help you with the heavy stuff? Four hands are better than two," he suggested.

Maggie was so excited for Jack's return that her better judgment flew away and she accepted his offer. Climbing up into his pickup and pushing aside some papers and cups that were scattered across the passenger seat, she sat down. Right away she realized her mistake as Tadlock reached over and placed his right hand territorially on her kneecap. Brushing it off, she turned to look out the passenger window and drew a deep breath. He was probably just a touchy feely guy, she told herself and tried to ignore the gesture. Things didn't get any better however when they went inside the country home. Right away he leaned into her—

"What in the–?"

Todd looked at her with longing as she pulled away. "I have been wanting you for the longest time, ever since the day we met, I just—"

Maggie was out the door and stumbling down the drive as she called her sister and asked her to come get her. Now!

She ran towards town, watching for Ali on every curve, staying as far off the road as she could. After a couple of minutes Todd pulled up and rolled down his window to plead for her to talk to him. Nothing doing. He was trying to save an unsavable situation. She spotted her sister flying down the road towards her and hurried to get into her minivan. Only then did she let the tears fall.

"Oh, Ali, I thought he was a little off, but he pushed way past the boundaries this time. We need to get over to the inn and talk to Kate and Dan."

As soon as they pulled up to Dan's place, Ali texted both of them to ask if they could break free for a moment. The request was so unusual that they both texted they would be back at the B&B ASAP.

Fifteen short minutes later the four of them sat down at the dining room table to talk. Kate could tell that something was way off. Her mom was trying hard to stifle tears. "What happened? Is it Jack?" she asked.

Maggie assured her, "No, Katie girl, he's fine." She gave them the lowdown.

"He's done here," Dan replied without hesitation. "Kate never did feel comfortable around him."

"That's a relief," Maggie relaxed. "But your deadline is so tight. What will you do?"

"We will figure that out, Mom." Kate took her mom's hand. "Somehow, we will get it done, but not with him anywhere around." Dan left the table and called Todd Tadlock asking him to meet him at the cafe right now.

Ali lingered to comfort her sister while Kate went to teach the noon yoga class. She managed to soothe her and remind her that it was over for Todd now and that Jack would be home tonight. They went back to Ali's until Maggie had returned to her normal self, then Ali dropped her off at home so she could get herself ready to go to the airport.

After class, Kate stopped over at the cafe to help Dan wrap up the lunch shift and prepare for the party that evening. She was relieved that Dan had fired Todd, even though she had no idea what they would now do about the inn. They would have to deal with that later, she supposed. And she knew in her heart things always work out. What was the saying? Things always work out in the end, and if it's not okay, it's not the end. Something like that. Maybe it was John Lennon who said it?

Five o'clock rolled around and Maggie stood nervously, yet happily at the baggage claim to reunite with Jack. He had only been away for a couple of weeks, but it seemed like two months in so many ways. Her heart was pounding so hard she wondered if it could be heard by those near her.

There he was, rounding the corner. She flew into his awaiting arms. They didn't let go for a long time. "You're really here," she managed to whisper.

"I'm really here," he hugged her tighter. "For good."

Once they arrived at the cafe, Maggie and Jack were thrilled to see the gang all there to welcome Jack home. The first thing that caught his eye was the welcoming banner the kids had made. It brought a big smile to his face and his heart was full to think of how much he belonged in Beacon now.

Surrounded by friends who felt like family, and family who felt like friends. What more could a guy want in life? And his favorite thing of all was the way his grandson J.J. jumped into his arms and held on so tightly. Neither one of them wanted to let go.

*   *   *

RECIPE (MY SISTER'S)

Cashew Aioli Spread

- 1 cup of cashews

- 2 T olive oil

- 3 cloves garlic

- 2 lemons juiced

- 1 t. Salt

- ½ c or more water

In a blender, mix all ingredients, add water slowly until desired consistency. If you add more water, it makes a great drizzle for soups.

Chapter 9

TUESDAY MORNING JACK STOPPED OVER at the cafe as soon as he could get there. He had made a decision the night before and was ready to run it by Dan. "Hey, Jack, what are you doing here so early this morning?" Dan greeted him as he came around from behind the counter. Asking Josh to take over for him so he could have a cup of coffee with Jack, Dan sat down to chat with him.

"I had trouble sleeping after Maggie explained what happened. I came up with a solution that I hope you will find agreeable. Since I'm a partner in the inn, and since I don't have to be back to the clinic until July, I want to become the general contractor until we can get the B&B ready. My leave was open-ended since we didn't know how long we would be in Haiti. Now it looks fortuitous that I came back earlier than expected. I am ready, willing, and I hope, able to throw myself into this project."

Dan didn't know what to say. "I can't ask you to do that."

"You didn't ask. I offered. So just say it's a deal."

Dan looked at Jack sitting across the table and shook his head. "I have been feeling overwhelmed, and now with Tadlock gone, I don't know what to do, but I don't think I can accept your offer."

"I don't see why not, Dan. I don't want to overstep, but I do want you to know that feeling overwhelmed seems natural to me. Believe me, as a doctor, I've been there. And often. I'm sorry to admit looking back that work took precedence too many times when I was married. Maybe I'm just old enough to realize it now, but if you are feeling like you are in over your head you might just want to get some help like I'm offering. You and Kate aren't even married yet, and I sure would like you to start off on the right foot."

"Man, I don't know. I don't want to admit that I'm trying to do too much. I want to pull it off."

"Haven't you heard the expression about things sometimes taking a village? I want to do this. Give me a chance, bud." Jack almost pleaded.

Dan was quiet for a few minutes. He reached across the table. "Deal." He sighed, conceding his need for help.

Jack chuckled, "Now what does a guy have to do to get breakfast around here?"

Dan stood up. "I'm on it."

Across the room at a table for two, Stacy and Norm were enjoying breakfast after taking the early yoga class next door. Anyone looking at the pair could see the sparks starting to flicker between them. Those who knew Norm hadn't seen the easy smile on his face for years, and it was refreshing to see the wonderful man relaxing with the newcomer. Stacy just radiated as she sipped her morning coffee. "I'm really settling into Beacon," she told Norm. "I can't believe how friendly everyone is. I can't walk down the street without someone waving at me. Houston wasn't like that for sure."

Norm laughed out loud and replied, "I have never lived anywhere else so the friendliness is normal to me, but I've heard so many others say that. It's the same when I go up to my place in the mountains."

"I didn't know you had a place in the mountains. Tell me about it."

"I inherited it, actually from my great aunt. The old mountain cabin has been in the family for three generations. When I was a kid we always spent our summers on Lake Lure. I'm not saying Beacon is as hot as Houston in the summer, but it gets steamy and just a couple of hours away the weather is surprisingly cooler. Our little town has a claim to fame too. Did you know that 'Dirty Dancing' was filmed there?"

"No way, I love that movie!" She glanced at her watch. "I could sit here all morning, but I've got to get to work. Thanks for breakfast, Norm." Stacy grabbed her purse and yoga mat. She sighed wistfully and started to leave.

"Before you go, I was wondering if you would like to go to dinner Friday night at Riggio's?"

"Love to," she turned to leave with a smile that she tried unsuccessfully to stifle.

Walking the short few blocks to her temporary nest at Dan's childhood home, she found herself smiling and waving at everyone she saw. There was something about Norm, but he was such a nice guy, he might just be friendly with everybody. She may be reading too much into the dinner invitation, but she had been stuffing down any chance for so long, moving to the next place without ever getting tied down or serious with anyone. Maybe it was time to finally stop running.

Kate waved back to Stacy as she sauntered over to meet Jenny for their standing coffee date. Once she passed the bookstore, she couldn't help thinking how much she wanted Reese to buy it and stay in Beacon. Greeting Jenny at the coffee shop door, she said as much to her best friend. As they took their seats after grabbing lattes, Jenny leaned toward Kate and told her she had heard about Dan having to fire Tadlock. "He always gave me the creeps when I came over."

"I know. Me too, but I didn't realize he would be that brazen with my mom. That was for sure the last straw. Mom was really shaken up. And on the same day that Jack came back. Thank God he did. The timing couldn't have been better."

She looked at Jenny then and her friend saw something sad in Kate's eyes. She could always spot what Kate might think she was hiding. "Are you okay?" she gently asked.

At that moment Reese came bounding in grinning from ear to ear. She joined her friends. "I'm so happy that you are both here. Dan thought that you–, oh, am I interrupting?"

"Not at all!" Jenny exclaimed. "Spill already."

"Brooks and I talked most of the night. We are both leaning towards moving back to Beacon. We even made one of those pro and con lists and there wasn't much on it to keep us in Virginia." They had awakened before the sun that morning and had taken a walk by Brooks's childhood home. It was only a few blocks away from Dan's place, down the road that eventually turned into Beacon Highway. After that stop, holding hands tightly they made their way across to the other side of the village and stood in front of the home where Reese was raised. Tears streaming down both their faces, they decided they could do it. They could go home again.

"Wow," Kate blurted, hugging Reese, "such great news!" She had been hoping they would, but thought it would take longer for them to decide.

"The timing is just so great. I actually have an appointment in a few minutes with Ruth before she opens the Book Nook. We are going to talk about the possibility of my eventually buying the store. Such a dream come true."

Amazing news, Kate thought. And said aloud, "Grab a coffee and sit down with us. There's room for three at this coffee klatch."

"Coffee klatch! Where did you get that? Are we eighty now?" Jenny giggled and said, "Why not?"

From now on the Tuesday am coffee klatch would be official.

Half an hour later as Reese left to meet with Ruth, Jenny brought up her question to Kate again. "You seem worried about something."

Kate hesitated. Nothing was really wrong. She just had the sense that Dan didn't have much time for the two of them lately. In her best moments she thought it was just all the external stuff he was dealing with. In her weaker moments, she worried that it might be more than that. "I just feel like Dan is a little distant," she admitted. "And I hope it's just everything he has going on."

"Kate," Jenny assured her, "I'm sure that's all it is,"

But she still saw the worry on her friend's face.

LATER THAT MORNING, Maggie and Jack were sitting on the front porch of his country home, enjoying their coffee on the warm April morning, mostly sitting quietly as they treasured the peaceful outdoor setting. Together. Maggie eventually broke the silence, "So do you really want to serve as general contractor for the inn?"

"I do, I'm sure there will be a tremendous learning curve, but it is something I really want to do. Seems like transitioning from Haiti to life back here, it will be a good endeavor before I go back to medical work. It's something I need to do for Kate and Dan. Matter of fact, as much as I love sitting here with you, I'd better get over there."

Once Dan and Jack had a chance to sit down and talk over what they should do next, Jack told Dan that he wanted to first check with all the sub-contractors that Tadlock had hired. "Let's see how many of them we can retain and go from there."

"Agreed." Dan said they would start there and see where things stood.

Chapter 10

JACK WAS FINDING IT MORE MANAGEABLE than he had thought it would be to serve as general contractor. And Brooks was in his post tax deadline time of year so he was proving to be a great help as well. And as it turned out, most of the subcontractors had issues with Tadlock, but were more than happy to work for Jack. A couple of them even officially hired Brooks to work with them. Today he was refinishing the banister and he found the work meditative in a good way after the mental work accounting required.

Reese popped her head around the corner of the living room to see if Brooks could take a break and discuss the possibility of purchasing the bookstore. They stepped out onto the porch. So much was going on inside the house that it was hard to think over all the construction noise. The quiet, gentle breeze reminded them of how different life was here compared to the havoc after the coastline storm that left their Virginia home a mess.

Brooks could tell they had some serious talking to do. He had been busy himself, but he knew that his wife had scarcely been home that week. From store opening to closing she had been shadowing Ruth, soaking in all she could. Reese told him excitedly, "I have been having a dream that I am trying to decode. I think my parents might be sending me a message. In my dream I am looking for my favorite book, and then I see my dad in his study poring over a novel, and my mom is snuggled in bed reading before turning out the lights. I go for a walk then, and I get caught in a bad storm. Once the storm passes I find myself at the bookstore. You are standing at the register holding a receipt that says something about my dreams, but I can't read it. And, babe, it's pretty dang real. I wonder if this isn't where we ought to spend part of our inheritance."

"Wow, that's some dream you had. And dreams can be really weird, but I guess they can maybe be messages of some kind too. Let's give it some more thought and see where we want to go with all of it." Brooks wanted the dream of owning a store to happen for her if they could work it out.

STACY WAS OUT SHOPPING WITH ALI for a dress to wear on her dinner date with Norm at Riggio's that night. The week had flown by and she had been so busy at work that Friday was the first chance she had even had to think about what she was going to wear. She wanted to look amazing. He usually saw her in sweaty yoga clothes, makeup free. Ali had good luck at Greenland's so they popped in there to see what they could find.

Grabbing three dresses from the rack, Stacy went into the dressing room to try them on. Two were a no-go, but the third one, a cream colored, long–sleeved, body-hugging, (but not too tight) dress, as comfortable as it was flattering, was the winner.

"That one is perfect," Ali remarked and told Stacy she had some jewelry that she was welcome to borrow. Stacy had a pair of wedge sandals that would complete the look so she was all set. She bought the dress and they went their separate ways so Ali could run some errands before the boys came home from school and Stacy walked home.

As she strolled along, her mind meandered back to some of her past romantic relationships.

After her disastrous early marriage, she had a few longish relationships over the years, not too many though. Her job and the way it kept her on the move had definitely factored in. She thought about the times that she would just start to hit it off with someone, but it would be time to move on to the next assignment. She started to let herself consider that it just might be different this time. One thing was certain. She was eager for their date.

DAN AND KATE WERE ENJOYING a rare moment together during the day. He had enough confidence in Josh to let him handle the cafe while he took the afternoon off. They took Freddie out to the dog park, sat on a bench, and just relaxed. As Freddie ran and ran, Dan and Kate sat on the bench and started talking about the wedding RSVPs that were coming back.

"The one that surprised me the most, I've got to say, is my dad's. He is actually making the trip from London and bringing as his plus one the woman he has been seeing."

"How do you feel about his coming?" Kate asked him.

"I'm surprised and pleased and worried and confused. All of it, I guess. I don't want him here unless he can come without creating drama."

"I get it. He hasn't given you much of a reason to feel otherwise. But maybe it will be good. There's always hope." They both sat quietly, each reflecting on how tough his dad had been on him. All that Dan had done over the years in an effort to please him. In so many ways he had influenced Dan's decisions that had kept him in a life that wasn't the right fit for him and away from Kate. But that was the past, and they still both hoped for a change of heart in Harold someday. Freddie interrupted their quiet thoughts, bounding back to remind them they were there for fun

Dan got a call from Jack asking if there was a good time to come by and talk with him and Kate. He sounded serious so Dan asked him if he wanted to come by the dog park. As it turned out, he was close by and said that he would swing over in a few minutes. Both Kate and Dan found themselves hoping nothing was going wrong at the future B&B.

When Jack arrived a few minutes later, he seemed really nervous, only causing their concerns to grow.

For just a beat though, because his nervous behavior turned out to be about something far better than the house. He was ready to ask Maggie to marry him and wanted, in a very sweet way, to ask their permission.

"Absolutely, we are thrilled for you two," Kate looked at Dan for confirmation.

"For sure!" Dan exclaimed. "As far as we can tell, you are the best thing that has happened to Maggie in a long, long time."

"Well, in that case, it is time to propose. Thanks for the warm acceptance, you two. Back to work for now," he was on his way to the inn to supervise the progress.

Watching him leave, Kate turned to ask Dan, "Hey, I just had a light-bulb kind of thought. What would you think about Jack and Mom getting married the same day as us? And here's what I'm thinking…we surprise Mom that day." Her wheels were spinning. "Like, we could enlist Ali's help and we could have a dress ready, and all her friends and family would be there, we'd have the setting, and–"

"Hmm, I don't know," Dan was the voice of reason. "How would we pull it off? And do you think Jack would be in? Lots to think about. Sure you want to share your day?"

"Definitely. Let's at least talk to Jack and Aunt Ali about it."

A FEW HOURS LATER NORM walked over to pick up Stacy for their date. Dressed up in chinos and a long-sleeved navy shirt, he wore comfortable leather loafers. He looked the part of a man on a first date. He had never expected to have another first kiss or first date in his life, having been happily married for so long, but life had ushered in a different plan. For the first time in over two years Norm was excited about his plans for the evening. His heart felt conflicted, and he wondered if he was dishonoring his late wife, but there was something special about Stacy. He just wanted to get to know her better. He told himself that it was just a dinner.

Inside her temporary digs, Stacy was dressed and adding the borrowed silver jewelry. Slipping into her sandals, she glanced at her image in the full-length mirror. Not bad for late forties, she supposed. Not one to fuss about her appearance much, she had put more than a little effort in tonight, styled her hair, applied mascara and eyeliner, blush and lipstick. She was ready to enjoy what she hoped would maybe be the start of something new. Could she open up this time or would it be like every other time since…

Good thing she was ready. There stood Norm ringing the doorbell. She opened the door to invite him in, but he just stood there. Dumbstruck was the word that came to mind. Then he smiled. Big. And said, "Oh my."

"Oh my?"

"Well, I have really only seen you in a hot yoga room, and, wow. You are stunning."

Stacy blushed. "You clean up pretty darn well yourself."

"Shall we go then? Such a beautiful night, I thought we'd walk."

He offered his arm and she gladly accepted. Off they went.

Chapter 11

JACK AND MAGGIE HAD SETTLED INTO the lovely habit of sitting on the front porch and enjoying each night's sunset, every one of them different and painted magically in broad brushstrokes across the sky. Both of them had busy daytime schedules so they treasured the nightly ritual, spent in the beauty of nature with each other. She rested her head on his shoulder.

"I could get used to this," she admitted. She had waited so many years to have this connection, this love.

"I sure hope so," he replied. "Actually, I'm planning on it. Do you want to walk down to the pond and watch tonight's sunset from the rowboat?"

Once they reached the boat, Jack gently guided her into a seat and carefully climbed in to join her. As they settled into the boat's bench seat, Maggie reflected on this newfound love and vowed to herself never to take him for granted. The pond was quiet and barely rippled tonight. She looked up above the treeline to admire the cotton candy colors revealed as the sun dipped behind the trees. She could not be more elated.

Whoa, maybe she could. She watched Jack pull a little velvet box out of his pocket. "I'd get down on one knee," he chuckled, "but I'm afraid if I tipped this boat over, it might ruin the moment." Gazing into her brown eyes now filled with tears, he asked her to marry him. "I never thought I would find this kind of love again. Please say you'll be mine forever," he managed through his own attempts to keep the tears from leaking.

"Nothing could make me happier," she responded and he slipped the simple, perfect diamond ring on her finger. They embraced, laughing with delight, and watched together in blissful silence as the sun faded beyond their pond.

Walking arm in arm back up the hill to the house, Jack asked Maggie when she would want to make it official. She told him that she didn't want to detract in any way from the kids' wedding. It was their time. So maybe they should marry quietly at the courthouse or wait until after Dan and Kate's wedding and have a simple ceremony themselves.

"I'd like the idea of a simple ceremony," he told her. They agreed to wait until after the kids' wedding.

"But I may not want to wait that long to move in here," she confessed.

"We are on the same page with that," Jack said. "I'm committed for life so the sooner the better. How about we see if we can get your house sold?"

"I think that it's time. As long as I can start bringing some of my favorite things in to make this home feel like both of us, I'm ready." She honestly never thought this kind of joy would come her way. And she was more than ready for the future to begin right this moment. Jack spontaneously picked her up and carried her the last few yards into their new home.

BACK AT RIGGIO'S, Stacy and Norm were having a relaxed dinner, discovering easy conversation and beginning to learn a little bit more about each other. They lingered over a bottle of Chateauneuf du Pape, which was Norm's favorite red, and soon to be Stacy's. She had never heard of that wine before. And she wondered about the price for a moment, but let it go. He must be able to afford it if it was his favorite.

They ordered the restaurant's signature bruschetta and decided to enjoy taking their time before ordering the main course. Julie Riggio had stopped by their table and encouraged the two of them to relax and linger. There would be no rush, no one waiting to take their table. She had reserved it for them for the evening. Norm didn't know how she instinctively knew to create that space for their date, but he was grateful to sit back and get to know Stacy better.

"So, kind of a random question maybe, but what are your thoughts on dogs?" He was nervous to ask her that in case her answer was that she was allergic or hated animals or something unthinkable as that. Three little westies owned a big part of his heart. They had provided such solace after he'd lost Barb, and now that the girls were away at school, they were his constant companions. Barb had actually rescued Pearl, the diva. Sterling and Toshi had joined the family just last year. They were siblings, and each had his own unique personality. Sterling was a cuddler, Toshi, an athlete. He was a great swimmer, and an even better ball player.

"Dogs! Love them. I was raised with rescues, and I have wanted my own for years, but it's hard with all the long work shifts, and then all the moving around. I just haven't figured out a way." Her eyes brightened, "Do you have a dog? Is there a picture on your phone?"

"Sure are. Lots on my phone. And actually, I have three." He scrolled through several adorable pics of Pearl, Toshi, and Sterling, then became animated as he told her all about them.

"I love that Pearl has a handbag with her picture on it," Stacy told him. "And I love that your wife rescued her. Tell me about Barb if it won't be too intrusive of me to ask," she gently suggested. She had heard that he had been deeply in love and just as deeply saddened to lose her.

He told her that they had married in their mid-twenties, having met in college, actually on the first day of freshman orientation. "They had us placed in the same group, and she was just such a pretty little gal, with the biggest smile. I thought she seemed shy. But then she came over and introduced herself to me!" Norm told Stacy that they hit it off immediately and really never dated anyone else again. She was an English major and he had majored in business. Norm went on to get his master's in business; she became a high school English teacher about a hundred miles away, and once he graduated and started earning a decent income, they married.

They moved to the home he now lives in. Charlotte was close enough for him to live in the charming small town and commute for work. Barb had grown up in a small town and fell in love with Beacon right from the start. She taught English at the high school until their first daughter Abby was born, now twenty years ago. Their youngest daughter Ava was almost nineteen. They were old enough to make it on their own, but still little girls in his eyes.

"Enough about me. How about you? Tell me your story." He wanted to know all about her. He really did. But he had been committed over the past two years to never getting romantically involved again, never needing more than his girls and dogs for company, never having his heart broken like that again. The girls and dogs would be enough. He'd had his one true love already. He'd been lucky, really.

"Oh, well, much different than yours, I'm afraid. I always thought I would settle down and marry, but once I became immersed in the visiting nurses' career, it just seemed to take me away from one place to another before I could get serious with anyone, or get attached to any location. I think I may have become a little too used to my independence. Somehow, it just feels different here. There is something about Beacon that feels like home to me."

Their waiter came by for their orders and they hadn't even glanced at the menus yet. Norm had eaten there for years and asked Stacy if he could order for both of them. She agreed. No one had ever ordered for her before. It felt romantic. She appreciated the gesture.

After a delicious pasta dinner Norm walked her home and they lingered at the front door. She invited him in for coffee, but he declined, gave her a quick hug and walked away towards his home. Stacy stood there thinking about how she had held back from telling him about her short-lived early marriage. She wasn't ready to talk to him about it. Talking about it made her relive it. She shoved the bad memories deeper inside.

KATE AND DAN WERE RELAXING on the front porch with Reese and Brooks. They had all gone out for pizza, then down the street to the local creamery. "So happy to have you two back for good," Kate said between bites of mint chip ice cream. "Now all that has to happen is for all the details to fall into place."

"Yup. And there's plenty of those details. Reese has to buy the bookstore, I need to work out of there after I apprentice here, we need to sell our Virginia home, and buy one here. Not too much, huh?" They all shared a laugh. Lots had to happen. All in good time, Brooks hoped.

Kate's phone pinged with a text from her mom, sent to her and Ali. Kind of unusual this late on a Friday night, it was a request for them to join her and Jack at the country house tomorrow for brunch or lunch. Would either one work for them? Kate shared the text with Dan.

"Sounds good to me. I have the cafe covered from mid-morning on, so I can go anytime." He wondered if Jack had already proposed. He could tell how ready he was that afternoon.

"I'm teaching the early morning class, so I'm good too. Wonder why the spontaneous invite?" Kate pondered aloud.

Just then Ali's response popped up on the phone. She and Justin were good from eleven on, so Kate responded that it would work for them too. She was looking forward to it. After glancing at her watch, she realized that she had better call it a night if she was going to be up to teaching the early yoga class. Saying her goodnights to Reese and Brooks, she whistled for Freddie, and Dan got up from his lawn chair to walk them home. They both had the same thought. Soon she would be there for good, and the nightly walk would be behind them.

Chapter 12

THAT SATURDAY MORNING Kate's yoga class was filled with the regulars: Tammy, Dale, Stacy, Norm, Jenny, Eunice, and about thirty others. Kate loved teaching the class. The energy and fun that everyone brought to the morning always started her weekend in a nice way. Norm's and Stacy's mats were in the center of the room. Kate couldn't help but notice that the two of them seemed even cozier this morning. Seeing Norm happy again was heartwarming. She hoped her Aunt Ali's friend would make the move to Beacon permanent.

After class she found a moment to talk with them as she cleaned up the room. Most of her weekend yogis lingered and chatted with each other after class. Today was no exception, and her favorite thing was watching Stacy and Norm laughing and playfully jabbing at each other. Their budding friendship seemed easy, like they were feeling comfortable with each other already. Especially now that Kate was happily in love, she wanted it for all her friends and family.

Speaking of which, Dan and Kate joined Ali and Justin at the country house for brunch with Maggie and Jack later in the morning and were captivated as always by the bucolic feel of the property. A light breeze blew in from the southwest and the sunny morning was a perfect 70 degrees. Maggie and Jack had set up an outdoor picnic next to the pond. It felt like a special occasion, especially since they were joined by Jack's daughters, their husbands and his little grandson, J.J.

And little did the guests know that it truly was a celebratory occasion. As soon as they were all gathered pondside, Maggie dramatically ran her left hand through her wind tousled pixie. Her diamond engagement ring sparkled brightly in the sun's light.

Jack's girls, standing alongside Kate and Ali, squealed in unison, jumping up to get a closer look at Maggie's ring. "Tell us about the proposal! Now we get why the impromptu brunch," daughters and sister exclaimed over each other. Kate stood there thinking about how generous Jen and Susan were about their father finding love a second time.

"Let's sit down to eat and we will tell you all about it," Jack invited them to the table and recapped the details he could share about last night. As the group munched on potato salad, waffle fries, burgers topped with over easy eggs, and Maggie's signature brownies, they popped a bottle of champagne and toasted the happy couple.

"When are you planning on tying the knot?" Dan asked.

"Not sure yet." Jack told them, "we either want to marry at the courthouse or wait until after yours and Kate's wedding. We aren't going to steal your thunder."

That comment was enough to prompt Kate to start thinking again of sharing their wedding day and surprising her mom. "Hey Aunt Ali, Susan, Jen, want to walk the property with me?" She gave her aunt and Jack's daughters a look that said she had something important to share. While the others cleaned up after the picnic, she told the three women about hers and Dan's idea to clue in Jack, but surprise her mom with a double wedding. She needed to know if Ali and Jack's daughters agreed.

Ali was pensive for a few moments, then blurted out some ideas of her own. "I could dig out my wedding dress. Maggie always loved it and she could wear it as something borrowed. For something blue she could carry blue hydrangeas, and for something old she could wear our mom's necklace. For something new–"

"So, you're on board?" Kate burst out, as Jen and Susan nodded their approval as well. "This is going to be amazing!" We just need to keep them from going to the courthouse. If Jack likes the idea, he can be in charge of that." The four of them linked arms and made their way back to the others.

LATER THAT AFTERNOON Maggie called her old friend Dee who ran a highly respected staging company in the Charlotte area. Dee and her husband David were two of Maggie's favorite people. She had introduced them to Jack back in January and could tell how much they approved of her new love. Maggie reminisced about the first time she had met Dee back when she used to take yoga classes in Charlotte, before she ever thought about becoming a teacher or owning her own studio.

She had been trying to pull herself out of her post-divorce funk without much success and the last thing on her mind back then was making a new friend. Ali had convinced her not only to give yoga a try, but also to get to know Ali's friend Dee. An Italian beauty with dark hair and darker eyes set in gorgeous olive skin, Dee had the curvaceous figure of a twenty-year-old. But it was her outgoing and engaging funny personality that shone the brightest. Maggie snickered as she remembered the first night that she, Ali, and Dee met to walk to an outdoor restaurant after a yoga class years ago. As the three of them walked to the bistro, Dee and Maggie hardly took a breath between sentences; whether either of them wanted a new friend or not, it was clear they were hitting it off. Over the years they had both been grateful to Ali for introducing them.

Dee answered the phone that afternoon and Maggie told her about her engagement and her decision to sell her over-a-century old craftsman home. "That's wonderful! I'm so happy for you, my friend," Dee responded, "about your engagement, that is. I hate to see you sell your home."

Terry Garrett

"I know. I never thought I would, but it's time. Jack bought a charming, peaceful place out in the country. We'll have you and David over soon, and I think you'll understand."

"What does your schedule look like for Monday? I could come over and take a look around four," Dee suggested.

"Four is perfect for me. I'd like you to see it with Kate's good friend, Jenny. She's my realtor. You remember her, I'm sure. If she can come at four, it's a date. I'll let you know if she can't. See you then."

THE FUTURE INN WAS ONCE AGAIN IN GOOD HANDS with Jack overseeing the subcontractors and Brooks working alongside, contributing whatever support he could. Kate and Dan felt like they could take a break from the wedding plans, the B&B, the cafe, and the yoga studio and just get outside to soak in the perfect late April weather. When they were in high school, they used to go fishing out at Dogwood park (Dan fishing, Kate reading), and today was ideal for Dan to fish and Kate to relax and read a feel-good escape novel. She grabbed the latest Hilderbrand, threw snacks into a bag, chilled some sodas and waters, and the two of them and Freddie took a day off to do virtually nothing.

Just a short drive out of Beacon, the verdant park was tucked away between residential neighborhoods in nearby Wesley Chapel. And it was filled with springtime blooms. Surrounded by dogwoods, red buds, glorious azaleas, daffodils, and pansies, they drank in the perfumed air. Snuggling in on a bench beside the pond, soothed by the center water fountain, somehow, they had the pond to themselves. Nearby at the playground kids shrieked with laughter, moms and dads sat back, and couples strolled the wooded paths, often accompanied by their dogs.

Since officially getting back together at Christmastime, life had been hectic. They both realized that they hadn't been taking time just to be together. As the day unfolded, they vowed to start prioritizing their relationship again. Days like this were going to happen, even if they had to be scheduled on their calendars. They'd heard from Jenny and Chris that it was hard for parents of young kids to even get out to dinner without talking about their kids. And they could relate to that a little, since they were always talking about the projects taking place in their lives. Today they just related to each other and let everything else go.

As they packed up to go home, Dan threw his arms around his future wife. "I love you so much. Today was just the reminder I needed that we need to carve out time just for us."

"Let's never lose that." Kate kissed him long and passionately. "I love you more." Freddie jumped between them to get some of the love for himself.

REESE AND BROOKS WERE SPENDING the afternoon at the B&B refinishing the tile in one of the upstairs bathrooms. They wanted to surprise their friends and to demonstrate how much they appreciated not only staying there, but ultimately, their role in bringing them back to Beacon. "Reese, are you ready to offer to buy Kate's house?"

"I say yes! But let's get our house on the market first. You know how ready I am," she wrapped her grout-filled hands around her husband.

"I know how much you want to buy her house and how much you want to own the bookstore. I put our house on the market last week 'as is'. We already have a cash offer."

"Brooks, that's amazing. You're amazing!" Tile grout be darned, she jumped into his arms.

"Have you told Dan?" she asked him.

"He's the only one who knows that I put our house on the market, but I think we ought to tell them that it's sold and we want to buy Kate's. Let's get cleaned up and take them out to dinner." Since it was a special occasion, they made reservations for 7 p.m. at Riggio's. Brooks sent a text to Dan so they would be home in time.

Maggie was over at Ali's helping her with a chair she was recovering so Jack ran over to the B&B to check on a couple of things that were nearing deadline. Kate and Dan were just returning from the park and took advantage of Jack being alone to talk to him about their idea for the double wedding.

"Jack," Dan patted him on the back, "Glad you're back here without Maggie."

Jack looked puzzled. That was a strange thing for Dan to say.

"Er, what Dan meant to say was that we have an idea we want to run by you," Kate assured him.

He sat down.

"What we want to propose is a double wedding. We want to surprise Mom if you like the idea as much as we do. And I had the thought when you told us you were going to propose, so after lunch on Saturday I ran the idea by Ali, Jen, and Susan. They all liked it. We thought Mom could wear Ali's wedding dress—" She was on a roll. She stopped to take a breath and Jack was able to get a word in.

"I know it's important to her that we not upstage you in any way." He was hesitant. It was tough for him to make the decision about something this important without Maggie's input.

"We know," Dan said, "but we think it would make our wedding even more special. Double the joy. Kate wants to share the day with Maggie. And all of your friends and family will be there. Just say you'll think about it, at least."

"I sure will." He started to warm to the idea. "And I could have a honeymoon planned for right after the wedding if you could work out the teaching schedule," he told Kate.

"We have plenty of subs that can cover her classes. That you would plan a honeymoon makes it an even better surprise, I love it." Kate knew there were plenty of teachers who would jump in and teach so Maggie could be whisked away on a honeymoon. That would make the surprise for her mom complete. She was beyond excited about it all.

Jack went back in the house to inspect whatever it was that he came to check on. Dan told Kate that he thought Jack would come around to the idea. "He's just the kind of guy that needs to mull things over for a while. Hey," he looked at his watch, "we'd better get cleaned up for dinner with Reese and Brooks."

"Freddie and I will head home now. See you in a few." She kissed him and thought for the umpteenth time that she could hardly wait to live in this house with him and quit going back and forth.

Once Kate and Freddie reached her bungalow, she realized how much she craved a soak in her beloved clawfoot tub. She would rather spend twenty minutes soaking in lavender Epsom salts than spend that same amount of time on her hair and makeup. She lit a jasmine candle, filled the tub to the brim, and sunk deeply into the hot water. Kate never understood people who preferred showers over baths. This was her respite, her relaxation. Immersed in the warmth, she kept one foot on the faucet in case she wanted to add more heat. Inhaling the jasmine and lavender, this was the way to cap off the afternoon and she was looking forward to an evening at her favorite restaurant with three of her favorite people. She grabbed her phone and searched for a country mix on YouTube. She turned the volume to high and laid the phone on the bath rug to keep it dry.

The bath felt amazing, but as she stepped out of the tub Kate thought about how awesome the day off with Dan had been. She found herself wishing that his schedule would allow for more opportunities to relax and reconnect, but she sure didn't want to add additional pressure by demanding more of his time and attention. What could she do to take some of the stress off him, she wondered.

A short twenty minutes later she was dressed in a pair of skinny jeans and a loose fitting white cotton summer sweater, threw on some ankle length boots, left her hair natural and loose, and added a swipe of shimmery lip gloss as a nod to the occasion.

As she and Freddie made their way back to Dan's house, she started looking forward to the dinner. Chianti, calamari, fettuccine alfredo, maybe some cannoli, yum; she hadn't realized how little she'd had to eat that day. Dan, Reese, and Brooks were ready to go when she returned, and they decided to walk the three blocks over to the restaurant. Tasking Freddie with guarding the house, they set out for dinner.

*   *   *

RECIPES

Potato salad (my niece Julie's)

One of those amazing recipes that you make by feel. You can't make it wrong

Cut up boiled potatoes, boiled eggs, several stalks of chopped celery, several chopped green onions, T or so of yellow mustard, Marzetti's slaw dressing–just enough to coat ingredients while tossing, mix in pepper to taste

So good!

Chocolate Caramel Brownies (my mother-in-law's)

- 40-60 light caramels

- A small can of evaporated milk

- ¾ c of butter, melted

- 1 c nuts

- One package german chocolate cake mix

- 1 c of chocolate chips

In heavy saucepan, combine caramels and ⅓ c of the evaporated milk

Cook over low heat stirring constantly until caramels dissolve

Set aside

Grease and flour 9 by 13 inch pan

Combine dry cake mix, butter, nuts and ⅓ c evap milk by hand and stir into dough

Press ⅔ mixture into pan, reserving remaining dough for topping

Bake 350 degrees for 6 minutes. Sprinkle chocolate chips onto baked crust.

Spread caramel mixture over chocolate chips

Crumble reserved dough over top

Return to oven and bake 15 to 18 minutes

Cool slightly and refrigerate for 30 minutes

Chapter 13

ONCE THE FOUR OF THEM WERE SETTLED into a booth by the window and enjoying chianti and antipasto, they all relaxed into easy conversation. Mike Riggio had stopped over to welcome them, and Kate was reminded once more of how delighted she was with their remodel after the fire at Christmastime, and the way the town had come together to wrap their collective arms around Mike and Julie.

Brooks interrupted her thoughts with his and Reese's big news before they even ordered their main courses. "We want to buy your house, Kate," he blurted out and looked at Kate and Dan, grinning.

"You're kidding, right?" Kate was shocked. "You are pranking me! Say he's not, Reese!"

"He's not! We love it, Brooks surprised me this afternoon with the information that our house in Virginia is sold. Already. So as much as we love hanging with you two, you could maybe get us out in time for your wedding. Sound good?" Reese was quick to act when she felt like it was the right thing to do. She and Brooks had been through the depths of suffering and now, most of the time, they found peace attainable. They have found it easier to live fully by just listening to their hearts.

Kate didn't reply right away. She caught Mike Riggio's eye. "Could we have a bottle of Veuve please? We are celebrating!"

She turned back to her friends. "We can talk about price and possession and everything else later with Jenny. I know we can work all that out between us. But right now, we are celebrating," she declared. "Not just that you're buying my house, but your official return to Beacon." Dan was almost speechless hearing the good news. Just this time last year he was still living in New York. Kate had no idea he was moving back. Life had become mundane, routine, and it was now just about as good as it gets.

The champagne was uncorked and poured. Dan raised his glass, "To unexpected, wonderful, and crazy life with great friends!" They clinked glasses and tried, probably unsuccessfully, not to overwhelm other diners with their exuberance.

"Let's talk about the bookstore." Kate wanted to hear how Reese's conversations with Ruth had been going.

"I have really enjoyed getting to know her. Did you know she grew up here and was a kid during the 50s? I have learned so much about Beacon that I never knew before. She grew up over Mary's Restaurant on North Main. Her dad was instrumental in starting the Methodist church and she told me stories about what a little town it was back then. You know that farm halfway up Broome? That was the edge of town in her day. She's a veritable fountain of information. And a lovely lady too."

"And?" Dan asked her.

"And what?" Her grin was that of a Cheshire cat.

"Are you planning to buy the bookstore?"

"Oh, that! We are getting close to a yes on it. I sure hope so. It would be a dream come true. If we get it, I want to change the name to O'Donnell

Book Nook to honor my parents." Brooks squeezed her hand, then picked up his menu. "Let's order, what do you all say?"

OVER AT NORM'S HOUSE things weren't as copacetic as they were at the restaurant. Norm's daughters were both students at Appalachian State. Abby was a junior this year, and Ava, a freshman. They were group texting him about his new relationship with Stacy. Word had reached the two of them that their dad was out for dinner Friday night and looked a little cozy with his date. Since their mom had died, the two, who had always been close to their parents, had become extremely protective of their dad. Up until now he hadn't dated anyone, so this was new territory for all of them.

Abby and Ava didn't want their dad to be lonely, but they also were not the least bit ready for him to start seeing someone. Intellectually they knew he might meet someone, date again. But their hearts still held tightly to the memories of their mom and dad together. Deep down, they wanted to go back to the way things were over two years ago and freeze life exactly as it was, their mom healthy, their dad and mom together. They were away at school and could pretend sometimes that life was the way it used to be, but not when they heard details from home.

Abby: Hey, Dad, we heard about your date at Riggio's

Ava: Yeah, what's up with that

Norm: Girls. I met a nice woman and we went out for dinner. I think you'll like her

Abby: You think we will *like* her

Ava: yeah, you want us to like, *meet* her?

Norm: yeah, as a matter of fact I do

Abby: okay dad, just don't do anything stupid til we do

Norm: got it. Study hard. Be good. Love you

Whoa, Norm hadn't expected to receive that group text tonight. He had just been relaxing out on the screen porch, admiring the sunset, and wishing Stacy was there to enjoy watching it with him. Hmm, his girls sounded a bit put off by the news. He guessed that was to be expected, but just knew when they met Stacy they would come around. He was actually thinking about inviting her up to Lake Lure in a couple of weeks when the girls finished up for the school year. Maybe they could all meet there so they could get to know each other. Sitting back, he wondered if he might be moving too fast. He felt so conflicted.

A FEW MILES OUT IN THE COUNTRY, Maggie and Jack were snuggling together on the porch swing, enjoying their nightly ritual of watching the sun set as well. Jack was thinking about the offer that Kate and Dan had made. So incredibly generous of them to want to share their wedding day, and he was starting to come around to the idea. He decided to find out if Maggie was ready to wait or if she wanted the courthouse wedding. "Hon, have you given it any more thought if you want to have a ceremony or go to the courthouse for our wedding? I don't want you to feel uncomfortable about living out here with me before we make it official."

"I have thought about it. It's kind of all I've been thinking about since you proposed." She glanced down to admire her engagement ring. "I guess I'm just old-fashioned enough to want to make it official before I move in. So, let's go with the courthouse if that's okay with you. Besides, I may sell my house soon. Dee is coming out to look at it and to give me some staging advice." She felt a twinge of sadness about the idea of not having family or friends celebrate with them, but she was willing to make the sacrifice so the kids' wedding plans and wedding could take center stage. After all, being married to Jack was the most important thing to her, not the ceremony itself.

"I like it about you that you're old-fashioned. Fine by me." He thought about the offer from Kate and Dan. Maybe they could still pull off the surprise afterwards. They could be married now and then be part of the ceremony too. And of course, the honeymoon would be a great surprise as well. He'd have to talk to Ali about where she thought her sister would most want to go.

"Let's not tell our kids until after Kate and Dan's wedding. Would that be okay with you?" She looked hopeful.

"I'd love for it to be our secret." Yup. He was going to be able to pull it off.

Chapter 14

JENNY WASN'T FREE ON MONDAY AFTERNOON, but she had assured Maggie that shouldn't keep her from meeting with Dee to go over staging ideas. Any staging they did would help her house to sell even faster. For her part, Dee was eager to give her friend ideas when she arrived at Maggie's, but the appointment was much more than a look-see to her. They sat out on the porch, catching up on each other's lives. "I can't remember a time that I have seen you this content," Dee told Maggie. She remembered when they had first met at the yoga studio in Charlotte all those years ago and Maggie had been a mere shell of who she was now. Love had a way of giving Maggie a youthful glow.

"I know. I was really struggling back then. We did have some fun anyway though, didn't we?"

"We absolutely did, and I am thrilled to be sitting with you here again. Let's take a walk through your welcoming home." She got up from her front porch chair, and opening the front door, started falling in love with Maggie's old craftsman all over again. "Maggie, you have just kept piling on the charm in this home. I remember liking it, but the feeling I get now as I walk in… I have to admit as much as we like living in Charlotte,

David and I have been toying with the idea of moving to Beacon, slowing down our lifestyle. We wonder if it just might be nice to experience every day the quaintness of it all."

"I had no idea. That's incredible. I would love to have you right here in town."

Even though Dee had the experience and magic of staging, when it came right down to it, she and Maggie had similar taste. Dee just wanted to move on to the kitchen and dining room to see if the feelings she was having about Maggie's house were real. Once through those two rooms, she turned to her friend, "I have to confess that if I love the rest of your home as much as I do so far, the only person I want to see this house is David."

"Oh my gosh," Maggie was thrilled at that unexpected turn. "That would be fantastic in so many ways. Not only would you live here in Beacon, but you would be here, in my house!" She impulsively threw her arms around her good friend. "Let me know if David wants to see it and we will have you two out to the country house for dinner. I've been wanting your input on the decorating ideas I have for mixing his things and mine."

Kate and Dan's wedding plans were going smoothly, but Dan wanted to talk about the amount of work he had gotten himself into. He had always felt like he worked better when he had lots of irons in the fire, but this time the fire might just be blazing a little out of his control, outside his comfort zone. "I'm thinking, Kate, that I may be in over my head with everything that's going on at the cafe and the B&B plans. I don't want this stress I'm under to overwhelm our relationship. I remember you telling me that I was taking on a lot with both businesses, and you have every right to tell me that you told me so. Anyway, I want us to come first so I'm thinking I need to get help so my only responsibilities will be cooking for the two places." He looked sheepish. "I know I've been distant and grumpy and even late to commitments we've made, and I'm sorry." He leaned against the new kitchen counter.

Kate had to agree. "You are absolutely right about that and we can figure this out together. Let's see, we need to cover all of your other responsibilities. I'd be happy to pitch in more, but I have enough to do with the yoga studio and the wedding right now. So we need a manager for this place. You can promote one of your employees at the cafe to manage there. Maybe Josh? If he is enjoying it, maybe he'd be interested. Also, we will need someone to run the day-to-day here, some staff to keep things running smoothly. How did we ever imagine you could handle all of it?" She allowed her words to blast out like a firehose. Just getting it all out in the open made it feel a bit more manageable. Apparently she had been waiting for him to open up so she could give him her input. It felt like relief just to be talking about it.

Reese and Brooks came into the kitchen and suggested they treat Kate and Dan to dinner at Mary's Restaurant. Brooks was eager to talk about an idea he had, and Reese wanted to eat there again after Ruth told her the story about living over the restaurant decades ago. Most of all they wanted to give Dan a break from cooking, to show their appreciation for being taken in, for the life changing events that had transpired since then. What seems like a small gesture can bring about big changes. LIfe really does boil down to making one little decision after another.

"Good idea. I'm hungry. Ready now?" Kate asked.

Walking over, they approached the Irish restaurant nestled just past the historic silver Beacon water tower. The ambiance called for Guinness, so Brooks ordered a pitcher and some crispy onion rings to share.

"This is getting to be a habit. I could sure get used to dinners out with y'all," Kate said while munching an onion ring, "What's up?"

Brooks stirred a little, seeming anxious, took a swig of Guinness, swallowed, and ventured, "I have a proposition. You know I'm planning to work from the back room at the bookstore, but what I really want to do is work for the B&B. I think I could handle the financials, the business side of things, I—"

Dan laughed and interrupted, "Like a manager, which it just so happens I am in the market for. Kate and I were just talking this afternoon about the fact that I need to back off and be the cook at both businesses. That's the part I love and really the only part I'm good at. So, what's crazy is you are just the guy I would trust to do it."

"Well, that's a relief. Let's order then. All of a sudden I'm starving," Brooks answered.

"First, let's make it official." Dan reached out his hand to shake Brooks's. "Manager."

Brooks, relieved, and excited said, "This calls for one more pitcher. It's a short walk home."

STACY WAS RELAXING WITH NORM on his screen porch after a double work shift. She groaned and propped up her tired feet on the couch. Norm started rubbing one of her arches, "I texted with my girls last night."

"Mmmm. That helps," she reacted to the foot massage, "How are things at App State?"

"As far as I know, fine. They'd heard through the small town grapevine about our date the other night," he dropped her foot. All of a sudden, it felt too intimate to him.

"And?" Stacy sat more upright.

Norm thought about the girls' comment that they'd heard the two of them were 'cozy'. He didn't want Stacy worried about their reaction. He knew how much it would mean to her that they like her. "I think they are a little, uh, interested in the idea that we are dating. It would probably be good for them to meet you. I was thinking we could all get together at the lake house in a couple of weeks where they could actually get to know you?"

That sounded wonderful to Stacy, but she'd better ask for time off sooner than later. "What would the dates be?"

"Let's see, May 5 and 6, that way the girls would be done with finals."

"I'll check into getting that weekend off." Stacy repositioned her feet so Norm could rub them again. She felt so at home with him. She hoped she got along as well with his daughters.

Chapter 15

DEE'S HUSBAND DAVID WAS AT HIS DESK in his office at UNC Charlotte, hard at work clearing the day's emails. Always too many for his liking. In his role as Associate Dean of Campus Life, he liked the paperwork part the least. A people person, David was best described as a guy with a friendly face and an even friendlier smile. He and Dee had been married for over thirty years and life was good. Their only son and his wife were expecting their first baby, a daughter. David was looking forward to becoming a grandpa.

He looked up to see who was at his office door and was pleasantly surprised to see Dee. The day had passed quickly and he didn't realize it was almost quitting time. Standing up, he scooted around his desk to wrap her up in a big bear hug. He could tell just by looking at the expression on her face that she was up to something. She had that look in her eyes; like a bulldog she would get something in her teeth and not give it up. He loved that about her.

She returned his smile and kissed him. "Are you ready to call it a day?"

"Looks like it's time."

Dee and David went out for dinner and she brought up Maggie's house. He knew she was up to something, but that surprised him.

"I can't describe the feeling I had in her house, David. As a stager I've entered hundreds of homes, but there is just something about Maggie's. I want you to see it. Just let me know when you can go and I'll let her know. She wants us to come out to their country house anyway, so we can combine the look with a nice visit."

"This week is busy. Can we try for Friday night?" he relented.

"Sure thing, hon, I'm on it."

"I was afraid of that." He slowly shook his head.

FRIDAY NIGHT WORKED GREAT for Maggie and Jack. Before they knew it the week had gone by in a whirl. They all met at Maggie's at 6 p.m. so there would be plenty of light out for the tour through the house and David would be able to see the beautifully landscaped backyard. All of a sudden Dee realized that she was holding her breath. She even had those first day of school butterflies flitting around in her stomach. She didn't know if she would be able to stand it if David didn't want it. After all, Charlotte was getting so big and they were both small town people at heart.

Once in their own car, following Jack and Maggie to the house in the country, she looked at her husband with expectation. He burst out laughing. "You were right. It is perfect for us," he admitted.

"Oh dear God," she realized she was still holding her breath. "I'm so relieved to hear you say that. Our furniture is already arranged in my head." She leaned over to kiss him. "More where that came from later," she promised with a twinkle in her eyes.

They followed Jack's car up the winding driveway to the stone house. Car windows down, the breeze blew honeysuckle, lilac and fresh mown grass scents into their car. Dee's gaze took in the pond and the red tinned roof, the welcoming front porch. She could hardly wait to get inside.

"This feels like peace," she told Maggie who whisked her inside as the guys pulled ice cold beers out of the front porch fridge and sat down on the expansive porch.

"Let me show you around," Maggie offered.

"I'd love that," Dee agreed. "But before you do, I just want you to know that your house is practically sold." She grinned from ear to ear.

The men were still kicking back on the porch. Jack brought up his and Maggie's courthouse plans. "The kids offered to me that I surprise Maggie and we all share a joint ceremony on their wedding day in June. I think it's a great idea, but Maggie doesn't want to move in here until we are officially hitched so we are going to slip off to the courthouse soon. I know we need a couple of witnesses and I thought it might be nice for you and Dee to stand up with us. That way we can pull the June wedding and make it 'official'," he said, drawing air quotes around the word.

"Whoa, that's a lot you've got going on. How do you think Maggie will be about not having the kids at the courthouse?"

"Not sure, but it's the only way I can think to pull off the surprise. I think it will be worth it."

The gals came outside then and told the men it was time to fire up the grill and cook the salmon, then went back inside to open a bottle of Sancerre.

"It makes me so happy that you want my house," Maggie told Dee, her face lighting up. "That takes so much worry off my mind since Jack and I are going to get married at the courthouse next week."

She sipped her Sancerre. "Maybe you two could stand up with us!"

"Oh, we would be so honored." Dee was sure David would be on board for that.

A few minutes later as they plated the arugula salad, spring peas, grilled salmon and oven roasted potatoes, Jack leaned over and whispered to Maggie that he had blurted out the offer for the two to act as witnesses for them.

"Great minds think alike," She surprised him. "I impulsively asked Dee the same thing!"

Jack felt the relief all the way down to his loafers. He was going to be able to surprise her. Now all he had to do was find out from her sister where he should plan their honeymoon. They laughed, hugged, and took dinner out to their awaiting friends.

WEDDING BELLS DIDN'T LITERALLY RING that next Wednesday morning, but Maggie Nola officially became Mrs. Jack Smith on what had to be one of the happiest moments of her life. Dressed in a simple white sheath, her short hair festively ringed with lily of the valley from the country yard, and holding the lovely bouquet that Dee had put together for her, she took a mental snapshot of the moment. Standing together in the stately red brick historic Union County Courthouse, she took in the handsome, kind, loving soul mate she was marrying. Marrying! Decked out in his finest navy suit, and wearing the best-looking smile she had ever seen, Jack said his vows, kissed her passionately, scooped her up into his arms, and swung her around the tiny room. She would never forget this perfect, defining moment of her life. A calm wave engulfed her being and she allowed herself to be literally carried away.

She wasn't about to let another day go by before she moved in with her husband. No matter how long it took for Dee and David to buy her house, she didn't care. She could actually take her time bringing out well loved furniture and special belongings to assimilate with Jack's belongings. She planned to enjoy every minute. Feeling like a young bride, as she stood on the lovely courthouse yard and looked out at the passersby in Monroe, she noticed that they were all going about their day as if it were an ordinary hump day. Funny how ordinary life goes on even when we are experiencing the extraordinary, whether it be happiness or tragedy. Shaking off the philosophical thoughts, she looked over at her husband and allowed herself to stay present and drink in the moment.

As they waved goodbye to Dee and David, Jack turned to his wife and winked, "Where to now, Mrs. Smith?"

"Home." She gazed into his beautiful blue eyes, filled with joy. Nowhere she would rather be.

REESE AND JENNY WERE MEETING over lattes at the coffee shop to go over the details to finalize the purchase of the Book Nook. Jenny looked over the paperwork one more time and then into her friend's eyes. "Ready? Everything looks to be in order."

"So ready," Reese said. "I have wanted to own a bookstore for so long. My happiest memories with my mom are centered around reading. My mom was part of a book club for as long as I can remember. My earliest memories are of sitting at the top of the stairs on the landing after I was supposed to be in bed, hearing the women discussing the characters like they were real. She and I spent hours at the library; when I was a little girl I went to story time there every week. Then I got to check out as many books as I could carry. Later I spent hours lingering, scouring the shelves at the very store that I am buying! Can hardly believe it. I think Mom and Dad would be proud of this investment."

A tear escaped and she just let it. She had learned over these past eight years to allow them to fall, wash over her, and heal. "O'Donnell Book Nook," she managed to say, "to honor them."

Across the room at the coffee shop, Norm and Stacy were huddled together over coffee and pastries in a back corner booth. They had walked over after yoga and were talking about their weekend plans for Lake Lure. Stacy told Norm she got the weekend off work so it was a go for her. She would have to work some doubles next week, but it would be worth it to spend the time with him and get to know his daughters. Stacy didn't even really feel nervous about meeting them. She had an innate confidence in herself and always looked at the bright side of pretty much any situation. All she really felt about the upcoming weekend was excitement. She loved adventures.

They made the plans and Norm tiptoed into the unknown waters of Stacy's past. To him it seemed like she showed up and lived life so big each moment that there was no past for her, only the present. The more he thought about it, though, the more he acknowledged that she did have a past, like everyone else. And he wanted to know how it had been for her. And he felt awkward bringing up the subject.

He came up with the words. "You know about my past, but I realized the other day that I don't really know much of anything personal about you. Just about your career and that it has you moving around a good deal."

She looked at him, took a bite of her chocolate croissant and asked him, "What do you want to know?"

He took a sip of coffee. "Anything and everything that you want to tell me." Just then his cell beeped with a work text. "Darn. Work. Going to have to wait a little longer." He hugged her, kissed her cheek and told her, "Sorry. Got to get on this."

"I understand. We'll talk later." Smiling, she returned the hug. As Norm left the shop, she let out a sigh and realized she felt a little relieved. She didn't relish talking about herself. Or her past. She didn't find any of her romantic history worth talking about.

Chapter 16

A FEW DAYS LATER WHILE MAGGIE MET WITH DEE to discuss details of the sale of her craftsman, Jack had the opportunity to meet with her sister to talk about where he might take Maggie on a honeymoon in June. The wedding was set for the 9th so ideally he wanted to leave the next morning and spend a week somewhere she would truly enjoy. Ali and Jack talked over lunch at the Ivy Cafe. They both ordered the soup and salad special. Today's offering was spinach salad and spring vegetable soup. They capped off the meal with Dan's signature lemon squares for dessert, and a couple glasses of herbal iced tea.

" I can hardly keep the secret," Ali confessed to Jack. "My sister is over the moon with happiness as it is, and when she finds out about the wedding ceremony and the honeymoon--she's going to explode with excitement. Nobody has ever done anything like this for her, not by a long shot. I'm so happy you two found each other."

"Not any happier than I am," he chuckled. "Have you given it any thought as to where you think she might enjoy going?" He took a bite of his salad and washed it down with the tea.

"I don't know if I have the best idea or not and I also want you to be as happy with it as she is. How do you feel about the beach?"

He swallowed his last spoonful of soup. "I think she would love it. The way she talks about your place at Carolina Beach, I know she loves to spend time on the coast. Where do you think she would want to go in June? I could talk to my sister about Cape Cod, but it is still a little cool there at that time of year."

"Well, before we go into the sand and surf idea any further, would you like it too?"

"Sure would. And you would be surprised at what an expert beachcomber I can be. I like to go out at sunrise. I can get lost for a couple of hours."

"Great. Here's what I think. You remembered that Justin and I have a place in Carolina Beach. You haven't been there yet?"

"No. Haven't yet."

"Well, Justin and I were talking about it, and we'd like to offer our place to you two for that week. It only takes about three hours to drive down there and once you're there, you'll find it quieter that early in the summer than it is in July or August. The boys will still be in school that week so we aren't planning to go until later in June anyway."

"How generous of you!"

"Wait. You have to know that it is a few blocks off the ocean and it is not a fancy place. I'm sure there are beach locations where you could go and be waited on hand and foot." She drew in a breath knowing that none of that mattered to Maggie, but she wanted to be sure that it didn't matter to Jack. It was his honeymoon too, after all.

She was hardly surprised, though, when he told her that he wasn't fussy either. What mattered to him was spending time with Maggie and what she had told him about the laidback times she'd had there had appealed to him. Maggie had told him about the "best donuts in North Carolina", the state park right on the edge of town, the boardwalk, the ice cream shop, and the beach stretching out for miles. She loved to read in a chair at the water's edge when she wasn't beachcombing. That would definitely be the place to go. He finished the lemon square, picking at the crust crumbs. "So generous of you to offer it to us, and yes." He thanked his sister-in-law, waved goodbye to Dan, and walked her to her car before returning to the B&B to oversee the reconstruction. Jack was pleased to see the progress being made on the upstairs bedrooms and baths. The kitchen was proving to be a little tricky, but mostly he felt good about the place. He felt certain it would be ready by early June.

ON FRIDAY AS STACY WAS PACKING for her weekend at Norm's lake house, she started thinking about the day they had met as she had been walking to the studio for the yin workshop. She was glad that she was the kind of person to dive into life headfirst. If she wasn't, she would not have signed up for the workshop, or been walking by his home just at the moment he was leaving for the same event. She didn't know if they would ever be more than casual companions, forever on the cusp of becoming a couple, but hey, a girl could hope. And she was hoping. She threw a sweatshirt into her suitcase and zipped it shut.

Driving up to Lake Lure the next morning, it was warm enough to put the top down on the convertible. Stacy loved feeling the breeze ruffling her hair and just let it blow wherever it wanted. Maybe next time she ought to grab a scarf before riding in the sports car. (If she was lucky enough for there to be a next time). This world of Norm's felt like a fairytale to her. Wining and dining, riding in his convertible to his lake house, relaxing with him and his three adorable dogs on his screen porch, she had to pinch herself that this was her life right now. She could never remember a time when she had felt this comfortable with someone, or this carefree. Norm glanced over at her as they slowed down to maneuver the switchback curves that spanned the last thirty miles. He told her that he hoped she could stomach the curves for the rest of the drive. She assured him that she was fine and relaxed to take in the countryside as the trees had filled out for summer and a little creek bubbled along on her side of the road.

As they slowed to pull up the gravel drive at the lake house, they spotted his daughters on the back porch. Their body language took the wind out of Norm's sails.

*   *   *

RECITES

Spring Vegetable Soup (quick and easy)

- 2 T. olive oil

- Large leek, trim and chop

- 2 chopped celery stalks

- 2 peeled carrots, sliced

- Salt

- Pepper

- 1 minced garlic clove

- 6 small red potatoes, quartered

- Small box frozen peas

- 4 c vegetable broth

- Italian seasoning or fresh herbs

- 1 can of your favorite beans

Directions:

- Cook leeks, celery, carrots in oil for about 5 minutes. Add garlic for one minute.

- Add red potatoes, peas, veggie broth, beans and simmer until potatoes are done.

- Add salt, pepper, and herbs to taste.

Lemon Squares

- 1 c butter, softened

- ½ c white sugar

- 2 c flour

- 4 eggs

- 1 ½ c white sugar

- ¼ c flour

- 2-3 lemons juiced, make sure you have ½ c juice

Preheat oven to 350 degrees

Blend softened butter, 2 c flour and ½ c sugar

Press into ungreased 9 by 13 pan

Bake for 15 to 20 minutes until firm and golden

Whisk the remaining 1 ½ c sugar, ¼ c flour, eggs and lemon juice

Pour over the baked crust

Bake for another 20 minutes. Allow them to cool before cutting

Chapter 17

ABBY AND AVA STOOD ON THE PORCH watching as their dad and Stacy pulled up the gravel drive. The girls could pass for twins from a distance and looked so much like Norm's late wife Barb. It always took his breath away as he was taken back to how Barb had looked when the two met in college. The girls were blond, blue-eyed and petite as his wife had been. When they smiled, the world was a more beautiful place. They weren't smiling now, however. Norm could tell by the way they held themselves close together, both with their arms crossed tightly over their chests, that they were bracing themselves, protecting their hearts.

He wondered if this had been a big mistake. Glancing over at Stacy, he thought she looked unaware. Of course, she was her usual happy self. She was open and welcoming and oblivious to his daughters' hesitancy. Well, there was nothing he could do about it now. He opened his car door and tried to pull off a smile.

Stacy got out as well, eager to meet Abby and Ava, and helped Norm grab the suitcases from the trunk. As she walked beside him while he pulled their luggage to the cabin, she noticed that they didn't seem very eager to meet her. She was going to find out in a minute that her hunch was correct.

Norm embraced his daughters and introduced Stacy. Her natural inclination was to greet new friends with a big hug, but both young women pulled back from her attempt and stretched out their hands in formal handshakes instead. "Oh, hi," Stacy managed, a little, no, a lot disappointed with their cold reception.

"Hi," the younger Ava said. Abby tried to force a smile. She didn't succeed.

Norm managed, "Let's get this luggage inside. Then, girls, I'll go out front and show Stacy the lake view." He escorted Stacy inside. His daughters remained on the back porch.

"Sorry," he whispered to Stacy. "That wasn't the welcome I was hoping for."

Stacy kept a stiff upper lip. "I think we just need to give them time. And I do understand. Let's go look at that lakeview you promised me and allow them some space. This has to feel weird to them." Norm felt relief at her comments and the two of them walked down the shaded lawn to the dock.

On the back porch Abby and Ava looked at each other. Abby was the oldest and knew she needed to at least give Stacy the benefit of the doubt. She grabbed Ava by the arm, "I don't think we handled that the best way for Dad."

"I know, but I'm not sure I can do much better. It doesn't feel right. I feel like he is betraying Mom. I can't help it." Ava fought back the tears that threatened to spill.

Norm and Stacy stood on the dock, inhaling the fresh pine scent and listening to waves lap the underside of the dock boards. To their left the view held mountains and to the right, a restaurant at the end of the lake. Across the lake, more houses. At least the view was incredible. "Let's go out for lunch," Norm offered. "I think you'll love that restaurant at the end of the lake. And it'll give the girls some time."

Stacy didn't have to be asked twice. They walked along the roadside to the Lake House Restaurant, nestled in the pines, a quaint log cabin that Norm told Stacy had the best she crab soup around. The weather was ideal for outdoor dining and the view included Norm's lake house. They were seated lakeside and Stacy drew her sweater around her shoulders to keep her warm as the balsam breeze kissed her cheeks, the sun warming her face. Even with the chilly greeting from Norm's daughters she couldn't help but relax into contentment on the restaurant deck with this man who intrigued her. She wanted to linger there, talking easily with Norm, and she felt somewhat uncomfortable about returning back to the cabin.

Once they returned, the chill was still in the air and Norm once again suggested an adventure. "Let me take you all out for a boat ride." Abby and Ava declined and said they were going into the small nearby mountain town to shop and grab some lunch of their own. Norm felt relief and disappointment at the same time. As much as he wanted this weekend to go well, he was starting to realize that might not be the case. He and Stacy left for the boat ride, both of them trying to shake off his daughters' attitudes and have as much fun as they could.

Climbing aboard the speedboat, Norm settled in behind the wheel and Stacy took the seat beside him. Being out on the water was always a cure for tension and it proved true for them that afternoon. Soon they relaxed into the sound of water lapping the sides of the boat as they slowly cruised the lake, enjoying the view of the houses that peeked out here and there among the trees. "I know it must be hard for you that Abby and Ava haven't been friendlier," Norm ventured. He felt bad for her that they were having a hard time, and honestly, he felt bad for them too. Maybe he had started dating too soon, but gosh, he liked this woman sitting beside him.

Stacy exhaled audibly and smiled back at Norm, "Deep down, I completely get it. I wanted them to like me right away, but I know that's not realistic. I can be patient." She reached for his hand and squeezed it, just for a second. She knew this must be hard for him as well.

Back at the house a couple of hours later, Norm suggested ordering a pizza for dinner and all of them sitting down afterwards to play a game of Rook. HIs daughters seemed disinterested, but agreed, and Stacy told him that she had no idea what Rook was, but she was game to learn. It turned out that the card game was a family tradition in Norm's family dating back to his grandfather's and grandmother's time. Abby said she would be Stacy's partner and she sat down to teach the game to Stacy. As they started talking with each other Abby seemed to forget for a while that she didn't want to like her dad's new friend..

Stacy was catching on to the game and suggested to Abby, "We have a little time before dinner. I love to make homemade pizza. Would you like to help me? It's so much more fun than takeout. We could grab what we need at the grocery store, then maybe all of us could make it together."

"I think that might be fun. Let's go," Abby agreed.

Once the two of them returned home with the ingredients, they invited Norm and Ava to pitch in. Norm quickly accepted. Ava stubbornly refused. The three of them had fun assembling and baking the pizzas. Norm opened a bottle of wine and turned up some music for them to enjoy while they worked. They danced around the tiny kitchen as the pizza baked and it really did seem that Abby and Stacy were starting to hit it off, but it was still apparent that Ava wanted nothing to do with her. She did sit down with them for dinner as the enticing smell of the pizza brought her around.

In spite of Ava's reticence, dinner was delicious and conversation started to flow. Stacy was glad she had offered the homemade pizza idea. It is hard to dislike some people when you experience their warmth up close.

THE NEXT AFTERNOON ABBY AND AVA waved goodbye to their dad and Stacy, deciding to linger a little longer to decompress after semester finals. Abby turned to her little sister, "Are you still really upset about Stacy?"

Ava tried to stop the threat of tears. "I, um, I don't want to like her." She was trying to forget how much fun it was to play the card game with her dad's new friend. I don't want him to get over Mom so soon."

Abby wrapped her arms around her, "I know, but she will never replace Mom. And he will never stop loving her. I just kinda liked seeing him laugh again."

DRIVING HOME, as he turned off the lake roads and back onto the interstate, Norm was unusually quiet. He was grateful that last night was fun after the shaky start yesterday afternoon. But he knew how hard it was for his daughters to see him with someone new. He felt conflicted. Stacy was a true delight, and he was happy to be with her, but was it too soon?

Stacy was lost in her own thoughts. She knew that Norm must be struggling with his girls' response to her. She had only had that short marriage and it was so long ago. What he must be feeling, she couldn't imagine. She might have to bide her time. She was more than willing to wait.

*   *   *

RECIPE (MY SISTER'S)

Homemade pizza. Makes two. You'll want a pizza peel and pizza stone.

- Crust

- 1 c. plus 2 T very warm water

- Add 1 package yeast

- 2 T. olive oil

- 1 t. sugar

- 1 t. salt

- 3 c. flour

Stir together and gently mix with your hands, if needed. Cover loosely with foil and let rest for about 2 hours.

When ready to make the pizzas, place the stone in the oven and set the temperature as hot as it will go. Liberally cover pizza peel and counter with flour. Roll out the dough as thin as you can, and add toppings. We like olive oil, fresh mozzarella, artichokes, red onion, kalamata olives, mini peppers, and baby spinach. Press them down well so they don't fall off when you slide the pizza from the peel to the hot stone. Carefully lift the pizza onto the peel and slide it onto the hot stone. Usually takes 5 to 7 minutes. Watch closely.

Add red pepper flakes and parmesan.

Chapter 18

NOW THAT DEE AND DAVID WERE BUYING HER HOME, Maggie found herself with free time to help Kate decorate the B&B. With a little over a month to go until the soft opening and the wedding, she and Kate sat down in the newly updated kitchen to make a plan. "Katie girl, I can see the stress in your face. Sometimes life is routine and everything seems to fall into place, but I know this is far from one of those times. What can I do to help?" She poured herself and Kate a cup of coffee from the new industrial strength coffee machine, and added a smidgen of hazelnut creamer to each mug.

"Mom," Kate broke down, "I don't know where to start. Everyone says that planning your wedding is one of the happiest times. This just isn't…" Tears flowed and she couldn't go on.

Maggie embraced her daughter and waited for her to empty herself of the overwhelming feelings. She brought Kate the paper towel roll to mop her face. "Let's see what we can do to get things back on track."

Kate nodded, wiped her tears with her shirt sleeve, and drank a sip of coffee. She managed a weak smile. "Where do we begin?"

"The yoga studio. Let's rework the schedule for this month so that you and I are both freed up. We have so many capable teachers who would love to take on more classes. I'll talk to everyone and we will line up the subbing schedule." She handed Kate a piece of the carrot cake that Dan had made the night before in the newly installed B&B oven. In between bites, she said, "Hopefully our students will want us back. We have amazing instructors. Yum. Carrot cake for breakfast. Yes, please." Shifting gears, "I think the next thing we need to talk about is Dan. Even though you have kept mum, I have eyes and I've seen the stress he's been under. Now that Jack is on board, and Brooks is stepping up to the plate, I think it would be good for the two of you to relax a bit and enjoy each other. Dan thought he could take on everything, but no one person can."

Kate nodded. Her eyes brightened. It felt good to have her mom acknowledge the stress and reality of all the day to day struggles. "I think we need more help."

"You do. I think you and I can handle the redecorating, but someone needs to oversee the guest bookings and handle the daily operations. I think I might know just the right person for the job."

Kate was all ears as Maggie explained that she had talked to Ali and Stacy the other day about Stacy's desire to put down roots. I think she'd be interested in working here. Can you imagine a more embracing, welcoming person to greet and host the guests?"

"No way, Mom, that would be amazing. I am going to talk with Dan right away about that possibility, and then, we could sit down and present the idea to Stacy." As they continued to troubleshoot, Kate could hardly wait to talk with Dan. Getting things off her chest and out into the light of day had lifted her spirits in a way that she hoped would also lift a burden off him.

LATE THAT AFTERNOON, as Dan was cooking their dinner in the new B&B kitchen, Kate could see his shoulders start to relax. He was finally cooking at home and not trying to do everything from the cafe. As he chopped onions, celery, and carrots, with lively music playing in the background, she brought up the possibility of Stacy coming to work for them, serving as host, kind of assistant manager. "I had a long talk with Mom this morning about our need for an assistant manager for daily operations. She mentioned that Stacy wants to settle down in Beacon and she sure does have the open personality–"

"She's perfect for the job," Dan interrupted. "He dumped the veggie combo into the oil sizzling in the fry pan. "She and Brooks would make the perfect team. Do you really think she'd be interested?"

"Only one way to find out."

Dan turned away from the stove to lock eyes with Kate. "Things might just be falling into place here." His grin said it all. One month before the wedding and he just might be himself again. Kate got up and wrapped her arms around his waist. She snuggled in tightly and relaxed into his warm back. Then she went over to the new wine fridge and opened a bottle of Sauvignon Blanc, the most refreshing springtime wine. Impulsively, she poured some of the wine into the fry pan and giggled as she poured some into Dan's mouth as well before grabbing a couple of wine glasses so they could sit down and have a sensible amount. "Let's call Stacy after dinner."

They decided to walk over and see Stacy instead, hoping they would find her at Norm's house or at Dan's childhood home. Hand in hand, they strolled down the street, eager to see if she would be interested in working for them. They hadn't walked a block before they ran into Stacy and Norm out for an after dinner walk themselves. Gosh, it felt good to see Norm so happy again.

"Hey, we were just on the way over to see you two," Kate told the pair. "Are you headed somewhere?"

"Nope, just out enjoying this weather and trying to walk off dinner," Stacy answered.

"We had something to run by you. Want to grab a table at the brewery and talk for a few minutes?"

Stacy and Norm looked at each other. "Sure," they replied in unison, both curious about what they wanted to discuss. Once they had a table at the old brick fire station turned brewery, they ordered prosecco from the tap. None of them felt like having an after dinner beer, but the prosecco tasted light and festive somehow on the warm evening. The big old fire station doors were opened wide to the outdoor night air. Sounds of laughter and lively conversation echoed inside and out. From their high-top table, the four of them had a great view of the B&B finally taking shape right across the street.

After some small talk, Kate broached the subject. "Stacy, my mom said you may be thinking of settling down in Beacon?"

Stacy answered Kate, but her eyes were resting on Norm, "I can't believe it after all these years of moving from job to job, place to place, I actually am." She looked across the table at Kate and Dan.

"I'm happy to hear you say that," Dan said. "And Maggie also thought you might just be the person that we are looking for to run the day-to-day operations at the B&B." He glanced at his house across the street..

"Wait, what!" Stacy shrieked more than replied. She could hardly believe her ears. There was nothing she would rather do. Looking at Kate and Dan, she calmed herself down. "Tell me more." She sat taller on her stool and tried to sound more professional.

Dan filled her in on the responsibilities, salary, hours, even an opportunity to live there if his dad ever came back to the house, and all Stacy could say was an emphatic yes. She didn't even need time to think about it. She did have to give two weeks' notice at the nursing home, but was willing to start working right away on her days off to help them have the inn up and running smoothly within the month.

* * *

RECIPE

Carrot cake

- 4 eggs

- 2 c sugar

- ½ c salad oil

- 3 c. grated carrots

- Mix above together well.

- Add

- 2 c. flour

- 1 t salt

- 3 t cinnamon

- 2 t baking soda

Bake at 325 for 40 minutes in a 9 by 13 in baking pan that is well greased

Allow the cake to cool.

Frost with a mixture of 8 oz cream cheese, ½ stick butter, box of powdered sugar and 1 t. vanilla and 1 c. chopped pecans

Chapter 19

JENNY AND CHRIS INVITED KATE AND DAN to take some time off that Friday night to go bowling with them, just to let off some steam and relax from all the stress that the past month had brought. Kate and Dan reluctantly agreed; they were both tired by the end of the week and honestly had been looking forward to just laying low. Neither of them had been bowling since they were in high school.

"Surprise!" Their friends, her mom, Jack, Ali and Justin, Norm and Stacy, and close yoga students all jumped up to greet them as they reached the lanes at the end of the alley. Kate's high school friends had been secretly planning a couples' shower to celebrate them. Breaking into groups of four, they took up eight lanes. So much fun, laughter, teasing, crummy bowling, and snacking happened at that end of the bowling alley. It was just the kind of evening that the engaged couple needed.

Kate and Dan were paired up to bowl with Shanti and Joe. As the evening went on, Kate noticed that Brad, their buddy from high school who now owned the bowling alley, seemed to have a little connection with Shanti that Kate had never noticed before. They had all been friends in high school, but Shanti and Brad had never been more than casual friends, not that Kate recollected anyway. She was sure that she would have remembered something like that. Joe seemed oblivious and so did Dan, but she was planning on saying something to Shanti later. What Kate didn't know was that as her girlfriends were planning the shower, Shanti's job was to connect with Brad and make the plans. Their encounters had left Shanti a little confused about her new feelings for her old friend.

Two lanes down Jenny and Chris were bowling with Amy and Andy. The two women were also paying a little attention to Shanti's seeming interest in Brad. Amy was never one to shy away from a little gossip. "Do you think there's something going on between those two?" she asked Jenny. She nodded her head their way.

"Probably not," Jenny responded. But the wheels were turning in her imagination. She looked over at Joe, who seemed clueless. "But I don't know. They sure are standing close to each other and there's something in the way she keeps giggling and reaching for his arm."

In the next lane over Ali shrieked and jumped up as she got a strike. The way she sounded, it wasn't something she was expecting. She plopped down next to Stacy and told her, "I never get a strike! Well, I hardly ever bowl. This is so much fun. We have to get out more often." Looking closer at Stacy she realized that she was not her usual bubbly self. "What's up? You don't seem to be yourself tonight. I can always see it in your eyes."

Stacy waited for Norm to take his turn and quietly whispered to her, "Norm's girls came home right before we left for here. It was another pretty cold reception when they found us together."

"Sorry to hear that," Ali consoled her. But by then Norm was back and their conversation didn't go any further. They changed the subject to Summerfest coming up over Memorial Day weekend.

Ali was deep in the weeds involved in the planning and thought Stacy might want to help get the B&B to be a part of it. She told her that Reese had plans to decorate the bookstore in red, white, and blue and to feature veteran themed and military books in the store window. The yoga studio would also be decked out in patriotic colors and offer discounts to veterans. In addition to that, there were plans for booths, a popular 5K run, food trucks, strawberry shortcake, cupcake decorating contests…It was a big annual celebration and occurred only a week before Kate and Dan's wedding.

Meanwhile the bowling merriment continued, and after opening their gifts, and getting themselves and all the wonderful presents back to the B&B, Kate asked Dan if he had seen what she had between Shanti and Brad. Dan looked at her like she was imagining things. "I think she and Joe are doing great," he said. "Your imagination must have run away with you. Brad seemed to be making sure we were all supplied with refreshments and having a great time." He sat back. "We have some amazing friends."

AT THE BOOKSTORE THE NEXT MORNING Reese and Ruth were finalizing the details of the sale with Jenny, working it out so that Ruth would stay as involved as she wanted, but the store would officially become the O'Donnell Book Nook. Reese was excited to hear that Ruth had a small staff who would want to stay on as well, including the summer help, none other than Abby Meade, Norm's daughter, who Reese babysat all those years ago. She would love to reconnect with her now that Abby was a young adult. In just a few days Abby would be working there for the summer.

Abby stopped in to see how things were going and to find out her work schedule for the next week. Ruth and Abby had become close over the years and were delighted to reunite after the school year. Reese and Abby were enjoying catching up as well.

The three women conversed easily as they stocked the bookshelves. Abby loved the bookstore, and she hung around to help even though she wasn't officially on the schedule yet. She wanted to get out of the house anyway. There was so much tension between her, Ava, and their dad now that he and Stacy were dating.

Ruth noticed that Abby didn't seem like her easy-going self and asked her if she had time to grab a cup of coffee next door and chat for a few minutes. Over the years she had come to feel like a grandmother to the girls and she didn't like seeing Abby out of sorts like that.

"Honey," Ruth sat down across the table from Abby, took a sip of coffee and placed a loving hand on hers, "how are things really?"

"Fine," She looked at Ruth, shaking her head gently, "really, fine."

Ruth sat there quietly, drinking her coffee, picking at her cream cheese danish, waiting for Abby to break the silence. She'd learned over the years that was the best way to discover the truth.

Abby looked up from her coffee cup. "Okay, I'm, uh, you've probably heard that Dad is dating. I'm trying to be good with it. Ava is too, but we are both having a hard time. And when we got home, she was at our house."

"You're talking about Stacy," Joyce said. "Have you spent any time with her and your dad, or was it just last night? I have heard a little, and from what I have heard, she sounds lovely."

"She is. Dad brought her to the lake house last weekend. It's not that. It's just…she's not Mom." She swallowed, fought back tears. "I actually had fun with her. We made homemade pizza together. She's easy to be with and she seems to be big on Dad."

"The hard thing might be that you and Ava feel like she is maybe taking your mom's place. She never could, you know. I do think your dad is still young and that a companion would bring him happiness. I like seeing a smile on his face again. But Abby, I am not trying to tell you how to feel."

Abby didn't say anything for a while. But she nodded. Ruth could tell she was thinking about it, maybe from her dad's perspective. Maybe for the first time.

THE MORNING FOUND STACY OUT FOR A LONG WALK. She didn't feel like she could go to her usual yoga class without crying her way through it. One thing that yoga had taught her was to recognize her feelings, feel them, then make her way through them without dumping them on someone else. To do that this morning, she needed a lot of alone time. The bright sun, gentle breeze, and mid-seventies temperatures felt good on her skin, but that was the only thing that felt good today.

Everyone saw Stacy as eager, happy to please, good-with-life kind of gal. And usually she was. But last night once again proved to her that she could get down in the dumps too. She had just felt like she could open up to Norm and tell him about her early abusive marriage when the girls walked in the house, home for the summer.

Once she and Norm returned from the bowling party, the tension was so oppressive that she couldn't stay in the house more than fifteen minutes. She had said quick goodbyes, went home, took a long bath, and crawled into bed.

Now she was out on this early morning walk, perfunctorily waving at every smiling face she saw, but her own smile was forced, and didn't reach her eyes. As she walked through the quaint downtown village on her way to the walking path on the edge of town, she spotted Abby and Ruth talking in the coffee shop. Abby and Ava were Norm's pride and joy. She could tell they were nice young women, but they sure didn't extend their kindness her way last night. Maybe she should stop seeing Norm, at least for the summer. She could let him have the time with them. Oh, but she didn't want to. Why did falling in love have to be this way, and after all these years alone? The longer she walked the clearer her mind became. This was the obvious solution. She would keep herself busy, working at the new job, finishing up at the nursing home, and she would wait out the summer, see what happened after he enjoyed a few months after spending an enjoyable summer with his daughters.

Once she reached his house she took a chance that Ava might be out as well. She knew Abby was talking with Ruth at the coffee shop. She needed to talk to Norm before she changed her mind.

Chapter 20

KATE AND MAGGIE WERE HARD AT WORK THAT MORNING putting finishing touches on the B&B guestrooms. They were both relieved to have their yoga classes covered for the month before the wedding. Marie had stepped up to temporarily manage the studio, their teachers were eager to take on more classes, and they were having fun with their second love of decorating. The rooms were taking shape, decorated with simple, comfortable, and welcoming in mind.

They'd had fun scouring estate sales, second hand stores, antique stores, even using items from Kate's house that she wouldn't need after moving into that very same house with Dan. They named the rooms: Quilt Room, White Room, Serenity Room, Family Room, Beacon Room, each with its own personality and style. Stacy could easily discuss the different options with guests when they called to make reservations, or they could choose which they preferred if they booked online. Each room was outfitted with fluffy guest robes, and would always have fresh flowers from the yard on the bureaus. Extra linens and blankets filled shelves in the closets and each room had a comfy place to sit and relax.

MEANWHILE, Stacy had found Norm alone at home and asked him if they could go for a drive, wanting to make sure they could be alone as she told him what she didn't want to tell him. They climbed into the convertible, Norm put the top down, and drove out of town onto a quiet country road. He was worried. She was too quiet. She seemed unhappy. The concern he felt manifested in his own mind, waiting for her to say something, anything. She finally did.

"Norm," her voice sounded shaky, "I need to talk to you about us."

He turned the car onto a gravel lane and pulled to a stop. He looked at her. "About us?"

"Yes. I can tell that Abby and Ava are not at all happy about us dating each other. And the last thing I want is to come between you and them, to put you in a tough bind." She drew a deep breath and exhaled slowly. "I've made the decision that we should stop seeing each other for at least the summer, to give you some time to be with them."

He looked at her in disbelief. "You made the decision, you say?"

A lone tear found its way down her cheek. "I did. For the summer. It's not what I want, but I think it is for the best."

He reached for her, but she recoiled. "I…just…can't. I can't come between you and them. Could we go back now, please?"

He reluctantly started the car and slowly drove back onto the highway to take her home. He didn't have the words to say, the words that might change her mind. So he just drove.

Once Norm dropped Stacy off, he pulled into his own driveway and sat in the car for what felt like hours before he went inside. Entering through the back door into the kitchen, he found Ava making a sandwich. Norm nodded hello and kept on walking until he reached the screen porch and sat down on his favorite wicker chair.

Ava finished making her BLT, then went out to see what was going on with her dad. "What's wrong?"

"Um, Stacy broke up with me, I guess."

"And you're sad about that, huh? Well, I'm sure it was for the best. It was too soon." She kissed the top of his head and went back in the house, dismissing his sadness.

Stacy could have moped around the Ivy house, but she knew that keeping busy would be the best way to get through her heartbreak. She went over to the B&B to start learning the ropes. Maggie showed her through the almost ready rooms and she knew she was going to be proud to host guests there. A feeling of hospitality and charm permeated the atmosphere. She felt sure that once the guests were there feasting on Dan's breakfasts and enjoying a respite after touring what Beacon had to offer, they would happily settle in and relax. Stacy sat down with Dan and Brooks to go over her job description. At least while she kept her mind occupied, she wasn't sulking about Norm.

KATE TOOK A BREAK FROM THE B&B to go on a walk with Shanti. The talking behind Shanti's back about her relationship with Joe and seeming flirtation with Brad wasn't sitting right with her. Shanti deserved to have a friend come out into the open with the concerns, not to gossip behind her back. Kate wasn't looking forward to bringing it up, but she didn't feel like she really had a choice at this point.

She really did believe that honesty is the best policy and hoped she could show love and tact when she talked with Shanti. The two of them were out in Mineral Springs at one of the best areas around for a beautiful walk in nature and they had just been exchanging small talk. Kate took a big breath and looked at her friend, "I have something I want to talk about, but I don't want to butt into your relationship with Joe. I don't think it's any of my business so if I am sticking my nose in where it doesn't belong–"

Shanti interrupted. "Kate, what is it already? Just tell me." She wore a concerned expression. "Well, some of us have noticed that you seem just more than a little, uh, interested in Brad." She exhaled, relieved to have the words out in the open.

Shanti stopped walking and went over to sit on a boulder. "Come here." She brushed the detritus off the rock. "Let's sit down for a minute. So everyone is talking about it? Does Joe think so too? He hasn't said anything to me I was hoping he wouldn't notice, I–"

"So there is something?" Kate asked.

"No, there isn't really. There almost was. And I was flirting with him. I just went home after the bowling party and sat with it all pretty much that whole night. I was feeling a little something for Brad and I didn't want to. So I let myself feel what I was feeling and then I started thinking about it. I came to the realization that I am in love with Joe, and it scares me. He's been married before, and he's been hurt and I don't know if he is in love with me or not, and…"

"So, wait, you are in love with Joe! That's awesome. He's such a great guy. Maybe he hasn't told you he loves you yet, but anyone with eyes can see that he's head over heels. How about you consider being the one to tell him first?"

Chapter 21

BEFORE THEY ALL KNEW IT, Summerfest was upon them and it was time to relax, celebrate the holiday, their small town, and each other. A sign in the corner of the yard welcomed guests to the Beacon Bed and Breakfast. Patriotic banners were draped above the windows in celebration of Memorial Day. The house was ready for tours; Stacy, Kate, Maggie, and Ali served the small plates of light refreshments that Dan prepared in the remodeled kitchen. Offering tasty tidbits to the guests who visited the house helped them to see what was most popular for the new menus. Town residents were also eager to get inside the old Wilson place and see the house restored to its original grandeur. Out-of-towners were excited to make reservations so they could come back and stay, chatting happily about which guest room they would prefer when they came to visit. They lingered on the patio, enjoying the shade the towering old oaks provided.

Earlier that morning, three hundred plus runners had pinned bib numbers to their tee shirts and ran or walked the 5K that started and ended between the brewery and the B&B. Finishers had found themselves under temporary tents gobbling up treats and downing ice-cold water or electrolyte replacement beverages, sweaty and happy to have finished the race, whether they ran for time or walked for fun. Kate had run fast enough to place third in the 25 to 29 year old age group. Maybe all that running with Freddie was keeping her in decent shape.

Nobody was going to go hungry in Beacon today. By mid-morning, food trucks lined the quieter streets that surrounded the quaint village, offering Carolina barbecue, tacos, pizzas, shaved ice, corn dogs, funnel cakes, and more. The bakery was running their annual cupcake decorating challenge. Jenny usually won. She was a whiz at cake decorating, a talent she had honed during her high school days. The strawberry shortcake was always a big hit as well.

Reese was hosting her grand opening at O'Donnell Book Nook. She and Abby and a couple more of the summer employees had been working hard to get everything set for the big weekend. Reese was holding raffles, featuring authors from the area who were there to autograph books, and she was serving refreshments from the coffee shop next door. The mayor was even present to cut the ribbon out in front when she opened for business that day.

The Ivy Cafe was packed from open to close. Josh had things under control. Dan was so grateful to have hired him to manage the restaurant. Even so, between the cafe and the B&B, Dan was as busy and content as he had ever been.

The weather was humid and nearing 85 degrees, but that was summer in North Carolina. Outside, visitors were standing on the old wooden bridge hoping to feel the gust of wind that would blow off their hats if the train came through below them. People were taking pictures of the iconic water tower and kids were getting their faces painted. Here and there on street corners, musicians played with guitar cases opened up to accept tips. It was small town fun at its best.

Stacy and Ali took a break from the inn, going out to enjoy some of the festivities. They hadn't had much time alone since Stacy had come to Beacon, and Ali was concerned about the sadness she could sense in Stacy.

She wanted to give her a fun day and the activities were certainly lined up for just that. Ali treated her to a strawberry shortcake and they sat in the shade of the village green to relax. Ali searched Stacy's eyes. "What's going on? You mentioned something about Norm's girls when we were bowling."

"I went for a long walk last Saturday morning and decided to break it off with Norm for the summer and let him enjoy the time with them home. The tension was too much."

"And you didn't tell me? All week?"

"I really can't talk about it yet. I miss him so much."

"Well, then," Ali hugged her. "We are going to spend the rest of this day taking in all that Summerfest has to offer us." She grabbed Stacy by the hand and ushered her over to the face painting booth. They promptly got in line with the kids to get their own faces adorned. Off they went after that to the bookstore to sign up for the raffles and to congratulate Reese. Lo and behold, there was Abby. Ali had forgotten that she worked there. They didn't stay but for a moment and went down the street to listen to corner musicians. Ali was determined to show Stacy a good time. The two of them giggled like schoolgirls as the hot sun started melting their painted faces into Picasso-like paintings.

Later that afternoon, things calmed down and it was time to close the bookstore after a successful grand opening. Reese asked Abby if they could sit down and talk. They had both skipped lunch so they made their way to the pizza truck and sat down to eat at a picnic table in the shade.

"I hope I'm not overstepping, and please tell me if I am, but I couldn't help but notice that you and Stacy were uncomfortable with each other when she stopped in earlier today." She paused and waited for Abby's cue to continue or shut her mouth.

"We, uh, we aren't so good with each other, but I don't mind talking to you about it. I'd welcome your perspective, actually. I have always looked up to you." She blushed as she gave Reese the compliment.

"Did something happen?" Reese asked. Abby told her about the weekend at Lake Lure, the fun they'd had making the pizza and playing Rook together, and told Reese that Ava was not cool about Stacy at all. And the longer she talked with Ava, the more she understood, and also didn't feel ready for Stacy to replace her mom.

Reese took a bite of her mushroom pizza, then a sip of her sweet tea. She spoke, carefully measuring her words. She knew how it felt to lose her mom. "I don't think anyone could ever replace your mom, and I don't know Stacy well, but she doesn't seem like the kind of woman who would try to. Eventually, though, she could maybe become a friend. Is there something you and Ava don't like about her, I mean, as the kind of person she is...the way she treats your dad?"

"No, she's a nice person and she seems to make my dad happy..."

They were interrupted as Brooks came over to join them. He had a plateful of pizza of his own. They would have to continue the conversation later. It would give Abby a chance to ponder what Reese had said.

THE NEXT NIGHT ABBY KNOCKED on Ava's bedroom door after Norm went to bed and asked if they could talk for a few minutes.

"Sure, what's up?" Ava invited her in. Abby looked around her sister's childhood bedroom. Not one thing had changed over the year she had been away. Hers had remained intact as well. She supposed her dad hadn't given it a thought. Left to his devices, their rooms would become like museum exhibits, nothing would ever be moved. Everything would stay frozen in time.

Abby sat. "I have been thinking about Dad. He is miserable. I think he really misses Stacy. He was feeling happy again. Maybe we are being selfish."

Ava grabbed her pillow and hugged it tightly to her stomach. She defended herself, "Abby, it doesn't have anything to do with us. She broke it off with him."

Abby placed her hands on her sister's shoulders and looked her in the eyes. "Because of us, Ava. She wanted him to have the summer with us, and the way we were treating her, she didn't feel welcome. I guess I don't blame her. We never gave her a chance. You know, Dad deserves to be happy. It doesn't mean he doesn't still love Mom. Think about it?" She hugged her sister and left the room. Ava always needed time.

Ava couldn't sleep and she went back in her mind to the time she and her mom had a conversation when her mom was really sick. Ava must have been sixteen. Her mom had told her that she wanted her dad to date again, and hoped that he would find happiness again someday. Ava had told her mom that she would never be ready for that. She recalled her mom's words. "Ava, that wouldn't please me. I want you two girls and your dad to find joy again. Promise me." And she had.

Two long hours later, Ava poked her head into her big sister's room. "You up?" She whispered.

Abby groggily replied that she was, barely. "I'll try to accept her, Abby. I'll at least be nice. I can do that."

Ava had started to think outside herself. Abby slept better knowing that.

THE NEXT MORNING Stacy entered the yoga class that she and Norm had been taking together. But now that she had decided to make Beacon her home, this running into each other was going to happen. She knew she had better get used to it.

There he was in the center of the room on his mat. Stacy didn't think he had seen her come in so she quietly made her way to the back corner and set up her mat. This definitely was not going to be her favorite yoga class ever.

Chapter 22

NORM CAME HOME AFTER THAT YOGA CLASS feeling despondent. His practice was strong and physically he was able to mold his body into the poses, but his breathing and focus were all over the place. He could tell that Stacy didn't think he saw her come in. Even if he hadn't seen her, he would have felt her presence. How could he not? He hadn't been able to keep from falling in love with her. And sure, he felt conflicted about finding someone new, but deep down he knew Barb would want him to find happiness again. He would have wanted it for her had it been the other way around. It is a sad fact of living that life goes on, but some of it can be glorious. Even if you never could have imagined it.

Norm decided to spend the day at nearby Cane Creek Park, hiking the trails, then sitting beside the quiet water. Whenever he needed time to himself, he got out into nature, and usually Cane Creek was the spot he chose. He couldn't count the days that he had spent there after Barb passed. He found his solace in the woods, the small lake, the solitude, the peaceful feeling that overtook him there. Today was no different. He had reached a decision. He would go home and tell Abby and Ava how much it would mean to him if they could somehow find a way to accept Stacy, or at the very least, accept that he enjoys spending time with her.

Driving the winding country roads home, convertible top down, the scent of Carolina pines filling the air, he felt as free as the summer breeze that ruffled his unkempt mop of hair. Sixties music blared from his car stereo, and he found himself singing along. This was a new feeling. This, he realized, he could get used to. Newfound happiness. And he was going to pursue it.

Once home, Norm braced himself for the conversation that he needed to have with his daughters, his grown daughters. He recognized that soon they would be going off to create lives of their own. They would make choices that he would need to accept. Today they would need to support him. He knew the trepidation that he felt was going to be worse than the actual conversation. It almost always was.

Ava and Abby were in the kitchen making dinner, music blaring in the background, dancing and belting out the tunes as they chopped vegetables and marinated shrimp. Finding the two of them preparing dinner and enjoying themselves so much, he decided to wait until after they had eaten the meal to speak his mind. Opening a bottle of chilled Sancerre, he poured a glass and sat down at the kitchen island to eat the cheese and crackers set out before him. "This is unexpected, but definitely welcome," he told his girls.

"What?" Abby teased. "You didn't know we could make dinner or you didn't think we would?"

"Both," he laughed.

"Well, we aren't completely doing it on our own. We need you to fire up the grill to do your part." Ava presented him with a platter of vegetables and shrimp, then playfully pushed him in the direction of the patio.

Norm took the platter and topped off his wine glass, and finding himself smiling again, he went out to the grill. He was going to enjoy this meal before having the chat, but after dinner, in no uncertain terms he would let them know that Stacy would be in his life. He would wait to spoil the mood until after they ate.

As it turned out, he would not be needing to spoil anyone's mood. In a poolside lounge chair next to the patio, all three dogs surrounding her as if in a portrait, sat Stacy. She grinned at him. There in khaki shorts and a white tee, flip flops on her feet, naturally wavy hair down, wearing very little makeup was the woman who had turned his world upside down. It was all he could do to set down the food and the wine without dropping it on the concrete.

"What...how...uh?" He managed no words.

"Your amazing daughters." She beamed at him and scooted the pups off her lap. She met him halfway. Throwing her arms around him, she told him. "Now I feel like I can tell you how much I care about you."

He gazed into her lovely brown eyes and found his voice. "Makes me really happy to hear you say that." He drew her into a big hug, and kissed her gently.

Abby and Ava yelled out from the screen porch, laughing, "Cook the food already!"

What a difference a day made.

After dinner Stacy and Norm sat out by the pool for hours. She was as happy as she had ever been but she knew, even if it spoiled everything, she would have to tell him that she was married for a short time. She hadn't found the moment that felt right, and this might not be the right one either. But he needed to know her deep, dark secret, the one that had kept her feeling unsafe in love, afraid to commit again. The past that had kept her running from job to job, town to town, until now. Now that she finally felt safe in love.

"Norm," she finally said, "I need to tell you something. I know you've been open about your past, but I haven't found the right time to tell you about mine. After college I was briefly married."

He took her hand in his, "Go on."

"It lasted less than two years. And it should have ended after the first month when the verbal abuse started, long before he was physically abusive.

I don't know why I didn't see him for who he was before that. He was my college boyfriend. We met in our senior year, and just after we graduated, we married. I thought I knew him. I hadn't seen the red flags. It was horrible. And I guess I've always felt ashamed in some kind of perverted way. I don't know."

"Oh, Stacy, that sounds like a nightmare. I don't even want to try to imagine the kind of guy that would treat you like that. You can tell me as much or as little as you want to, for the rest of our lives. But it will never be an issue that affects our relationship. I will only treasure you. As long as I live." He kissed her tenderly. And she knew it was true. And real.

Chapter 23

JACK AND MAGGIE WERE HARD AT WORK at their country home preparing for the rehearsal dinner to be held there in just two days. They had been busy mixing in as many of her belongings as they could with his so that her house could be ready for Dee and David to move in. Surprisingly, it hadn't been as difficult as they thought it might be. Both of them were easygoing about what they kept and what they didn't. Luckily for them, the sprawling lodge held plenty of furnishings.

Outside they were overseeing the set up of a circus-sized tent next to the pond where they would host the dinner on Friday night. Jack's sister, Mimi, and her husband Jon had arrived from their home in Cape Cod and were pitching in like it was their job. They were well qualified to help. On the edge of the ocean at the elbow of the cape, they owned and operated a mansion-sized B&B. Mimi was a natural at decorating and hosting. Maggie stood and admired her new sister-in-law for a moment. The two of them were almost the same age, but Mimi had the vitality of a woman two decades younger. She wore her thick brunette hair long, usually didn't apply a trace of makeup, and was such a healthy eater that her figure was trim as it ever had been. She rarely sat down.

Between the four of them, the last minute details were finalized with food trucks that would be parked beside the tent. They went over the decorations and flowers and candle lighting again with Tammy.

They arranged for their friends and favorite duo, Danika and the Jeb, who were going to sing at the wedding, to also play background music for the rehearsal dinner. Seating arrangements had been planned and place cards were being handwritten by Jack, whose largely unknown side talent was calligraphy. The weather all week promised to be warm, bordering on hot, with sunny skies. And the night of the rehearsal, a full moon would shed its light over the pond.

Jack decided late that night to give Maggie the surprising news about the double wedding. He could hardly believe that he had been able to keep it from her until now. They were finally out alone on the front porch swing, the only light from the moon, and he leaned in. "Mags," he began. "I have a surprise for you."

She perked up. "I love surprises! Where is it?"

"It's more of an announcement than a thing." He beamed. "A while back the kids told me they wanted us to share in their wedding–"

"I know, Jack. I'm so excited to be walking Kate down the aisle."

"Well, the thing is, you can still do that. But after they are pronounced husband and wife, you will be walking down the aisle alone, in Ali's wedding dress, to me. They've planned a double wedding and I am excited to tell you–"

Maggie's face fell. Jack could see it in the moonlight. Downcast. He was shocked. She didn't want this. "Honey, I'm…I know you expected me to be joyful. I'm sure Dan and Kate did too. And Ali, and whoever else is involved, but why didn't anyone think to include me in this plan? I hate it. I want this wedding to be Kate and Dan's alone." She was brutally honest. And sad, and angry. He'd never seen her so angry. They sat in silence. The only sounds were pond water lapping the shore, and the overhead owl, locusts, and crickets. Silence otherwise. Uncomfortable silence.

Mimi, unaware of the serious conversation, stepped out on the porch. "Jon and I were wondering if you would like a cup of chamomile tea? I have the teapot going." She looked at them, squinted in the darkness to search their faces. "What's wrong?" she asked.

Maggie attempted to sound lighthearted. "We were just talking about wedding logistics."

Jack told his sister, "We just need to work out a couple of those issues, so maybe we could take a raincheck on the tea." Mimi could tell by the strain in his voice that something was not quite right, and nodding her agreement, she backed into the house.

Maggie turned to face her husband. She drew in a big breath, then stated her piece. "I can't believe that none of you thought that I would want a say in something this big. I just can't."

She got up and went inside. Jack was bereft. He could only sit there.

Maggie, breaking through the front door, literally ran into Mimi.

Mimi didn't know Maggie well, but she knew enough to know that she was a perfect match for her brother and she sure didn't like seeing how upset she was. "If you want a listening ear, I'm here," she offered. "How about we sit down at the kitchen table and I pour you a cup of the comforting tea?"

Maggie nodded affirmatively, accepting her offer. She sat down at the banquette and hugged one of the throw pillows tightly against her. Mimi sat down beside her and wordlessly placed the cup of tea in front of her. Maggie confessed to her new sister-in-law, "I don't want to speak badly about your brother."

"I don't see it that way," Mimi shared. "Jon and I have been married almost thirty years and there have been plenty of disagreements over those decades. I have a sneaky suspicion this may have been your first major argument."

"I guess it was. Jack, Kate, Dan, and my sister thought it would be a good idea to surprise me and had planned that Jack and I would be married at the same time in a double wedding. Evidently nobody thought it would be a good idea to get my opinion on the matter. There is no way I am going to overshadow my daughter's wedding by getting married at the same time." She hugged the pillow so tightly that Mimi thought the stuffing might pop out.

"I can see why that would be upsetting to you. Sounds like they thought it would be something you would want; I can't imagine all those loved ones intentionally wanting to upset you. But I can see why you would want to be consulted." She took a sip of the chamomile tea and waited for Maggie to respond.

Maggie put down her mug and said, " When you put it that way, it seems like I may have overreacted. Probably hurt Jack's feelings. I know he thought it would be a wonderful surprise. The big problem is that I don't want it. At all."

Just then Jack came into the kitchen and poured himself a cup of water. Immersing the tea bag into his mug, he asked, "Is this a private conversation or can I sit down with you?"

"You're more than welcome," Maggie smiled weakly. Mimi stood up and said goodnight, kissing them both on their cheeks before leaving the two of them alone to work things out. Jack got up and moved over to sit next to his wife on the banquette.

'I'm so sorry that I took the liberty of saying yes for both of us," he gently placed his hand on Maggie's. "I don't like having such a big thing between us, and it was stupid of me to think it would be a good idea surprising you on something this big." He searched her eyes.

She sat quietly, drinking her tea, but he noticed that she released her tight grip on the throw pillow. Reaching for his hand after what seemed to Jack an eternity, she finally spoke, "I love you, Jack, but I guess we will still face disagreements. We just hadn't until now, and I think I unrealistically thought we never would. So silly of me."

"Not silly. But yeah, unrealistic. And this one is a big deal. And I get that you don't want to upstage their wedding in any way."

"No. I don't." She looked down at her tea mug like there was some kind of magic answer there. "I need to talk to my daughter first thing tomorrow. Let's get some sleep."

Chapter 24

NOW THAT THE BEACON B&B was ready for the soft opening, and would be hosting wedding guests over the next couple of days, Brooks and Reese were busy moving out of their temporary room just off the kitchen, and finally getting into their new house. It felt like a smooth transition, moving a few blocks away to Kate's bungalow, kind of a switcheroo, Kate's belongings making their way into her new home, and theirs going to hers.

Reese and Brooks could still hardly believe the turn their lives had taken. Moving back had been a big step, but everything had unfolded so smoothly. Sometimes they wondered how much his grandma and her parents were helping to orchestrate their lives. Their devastating losses eight years ago had impacted them in unbelievable ways. Of course, they had been changed as they made their way through the grief and crawled forward into their new lives. It had made them closer instead of pulling them apart. For that they were both immensely grateful.

Reese glanced over at her husband as they packed up their belongings. He was so much happier being busily involved in the financial affairs of the inn. She realized how much better off he was now that his work offered him personal connections. And how much Reese, too, enjoyed the interactions she had with old friends and new at the bookstore. This move had proven to be a good one. She was excited about the future. And for good reason. The pregnancy test she took that morning had come back positive. She was trying to come up with a special way to tell Brooks.

Kate heard them working and stopped in to see if they could use her help. "Knock, knock, what can I do to make the move easier for you two?" She slowly pushed open the door and found them busy packing.

"Are you crazy?" Brooks asked her. "Two days before your wedding and you are offering us help? I don't think so. We are good." He shook his head in disbelief.

Kate started to protest, but her cell phone rang. "Hi Mom," she answered.

"Hi, how are things going over there?" Her mom's voice sounded off to her.

Kate waved silently to Brooks and Reese, backing out of the room and into the kitchen. "I was just trying to see if I could help B and R move out, but they seem to have it covered."

"Glad to hear that. You have some free time this morning then? I wanted to go on that hike that we used to take together over the suspension bridge into South Carolina. Can you spare the morning for old time's sake?"

Kate had a million things she could be doing but the temptation to take that walk with her mom on such a pretty spring morning took precedence. "How about I meet you in the parking lot by the school in half an hour?"

"See you then." Her mom hung up.

Kate ran home to change into lightweight hiking clothes, liberally applied sunscreen, and grabbed Freddie for the hike. When she met her mom and the two of them got out of their cars, she could tell something was wrong. This wasn't going to be a comfortable hike, in more ways than one. It was getting hot, the hike was hilly through the woods, and something was bothering Maggie.

After bending down to ruffle Freddie's fur, Maggie set off to walk through the neighborhood to the hiking trail, Kate just behind her. "Remember back in the day, when this school wasn't here, this neighborhood wasn't either, and all there was…nature all around us. Things sure do have a way of changing; time definitely marches on." Maggie was feeling sentimental and at the same time, uneasy about the talk she needed to have with Kate. She didn't want to upset her, but she also didn't want the double wedding plans.

The two walked on, side by side, Freddie running ahead. Maggie dipped her proverbial toe into the murky water. "Hon, Jack told me last night about the double wedding surprise." Kate looked sideways at her mom's expression. She didn't look happy about the plans. Not in the least.

"And? You aren't happy about it?"

Quietly her mom replied, "No. Sorry, I'm not. I will not have you sharing your wedding day with me."

"You sound pretty definite." Kate could tell that her mom meant it. They walked on, reaching the suspension bridge that hung over the state line. It looked to Kate as if her mom was drawing a line of her own.

"I am overjoyed to walk you down the aisle," Maggie turned to take in the view from the bridge. "And there's more. Let's go sit on that bench over there so we can talk."

Freddie came bounding back once he realized that they weren't behind him. Kate got out the water bowl she'd brought in her backpack and filled it for him. "Okay, Mom, tell me."

Maggie swatted at a mosquito and started to divulge her own secret. "Jack and I got married at the courthouse a couple of weeks ago, before I moved into his house."

"You…you.. what?" Kate quizzed her. "You got married already? Without me there? Was Ali there? Jack's daughters?"

"No. None of you. I got so caught up in the moment. Jack had asked if I wanted a ceremony or to just go to the courthouse. I wanted so badly to be with him, but not until we were married, so I said courthouse. It was so important to me that you kids get your wedding without us upstaging you that I asked him if we could keep it a secret until after you were married. When I look back at it logically it makes no sense to me either. I would go back and change that in a heartbeat if I could. I feel so sorry. And I have to admit, ashamed. I let you and Ali down. He let his daughters down. It was like we were teenagers." She had let the words spill out, directly from her heart. But she stared out at the woods as she told her. She couldn't face her daughter.

"Oh, mom, I'm really hurt. And I'm trying to understand. But right now I think I need some time."

"I understand." Maggie looked down at the ground.

"So who were your witnesses?"

"Dee and David. We knew they could keep it a secret."

Katie looked at her mom in sincere disbelief. "I need some time." She reached for Freddie's leash, put his bowl back in her backpack. "I think I'm just going to go back now. I love you, Mom, but I need to process this."

Maggie watched them walk back across the bridge to the North Carolina side. Then she just sat there and let the tears flow. For a long time.

Chapter 25

REESE AND BROOKS WERE MOVING SOME OF THEIR BOXES into Kate's house that afternoon. He teased her about the light loads she was carrying. She laughed and asked him to open the door to the little bedroom across the hall from the master.

"Let's set this down here."

"Why in here?"

"Because this will be the baby's room." She was glowing.

"But not for a —"

"Sooner than you think." She pulled the positive test out of the box she had just placed on the floor.

"So we're–?"

"Yes, Brooks. We are!" She placed his hand on her flat belly. He kissed her tenderly, then wrapped her up in a tight embrace and kissed her anything but tenderly. The moment felt like magic.

KATE HAD DRIVEN TO HER AUNT ALI'S HOUSE and showed up on her doorstep visibly shaken. Cheydon opened the door to find his cousin standing there with Freddie, obviously upset. He stared into her eyes while yelling out, "Mom, come to the front door. Kate needs you!" Then he opened the door to let them in. It was the best the sixteen year old could manage. He'd never seen Kate that upset before.

Ali made her way to the doorway and wrapped Kate up in a hug. "What's wrong, Katie girl?"

"I was just with Mom—"

"Tell me she's okay." Ali demanded.

"She's okay, but she told me she got married at the county court-house, and on top of that, she hates the idea of the double wedding!"

Ali let out a deep sigh of relief. "Come sit down on the front porch with me. Cheydon, please go pour us a couple of glasses of sweet tea." She led her niece to the wicker chairs. "Kate, tell me what happened. Did you talk to your mom?"

"We went for a walk this morning." She paused to thank Cheydon and took the iced tea from him. Ali was calming her nerves. She let the story spill out, petting Freddie as she talked.

Ali drank her tea while she listened. Once Kate had told her the whole story, she responded, probably not with the words that Kate expected to hear. "I bet your mom feels awful. Where is she?"

"I left her on the bench. On the South Carolina side of the suspension bridge. Why are you talking about how she feels?"

"Because this behavior of getting married without us there, it's not characteristic of her. She must have felt awful once she realized what she did, what she got caught up in. I'm not saying that I don't wish I'd been there," she measured her words, "but I think we did act presumptuously planning her wedding for her. I know Jack had plans to surprise her for a honeymoon and they are just so right for each other. I am so glad she is finally happy again."

"I want her to be happy too. It's just that I feel so left out. He mentioned something back when he was planning to propose about a honeymoon surprise. Did he share the details of where they were going with you?"

"Oh, Jack asked me where your mom would want to go on a honeymoon and I offered the beach house. I think she will like that surprise."

"She will. It's perfect. And I am excited for her." Kate sat there without saying anything else for about ten minutes. "You know what?" She said to her aunt, "I love you so much, and I'm going to go find Mom."

"Oh, Katie girl, I love you too. Go!"

Kate sat in the car and called her mom. "Where are you?"

Maggie told her she had just hiked back to the parking lot and was getting into her car. "Stay there. Please. Freddie and I are on our way back." She hung up so her mom couldn't refuse. Once back to the parking lot, Kate got out of her car and into her mom's. "I'm getting married in two days. Time for happiness. I love you." She reached across the center console to give her mom a hug.

THAT AFTERNOON FOUND THE BEACON B&B springing to life. Stacy greeted Dan and Kate's families and friends as they arrived to check in for the wedding festivities. She was planning to stay there as well since Harold Ivy and his girlfriend were arriving that afternoon. Dan left to pick them up from the Charlotte airport.

Dan's dad had been away since last Thanksgiving for the most part. Their relationship had been strained for as long as Dan could remember. He was anxious to meet his dad's new girlfriend though. He'd not had many conversations with his dad over the past few months, yet somehow when they did talk the tension didn't feel quite as bad as it had in the past.

Once Dan arrived, he waited in the cell phone lot until they'd been able to get through customs. They'd be out soon.

Diane walked out ahead of Harold, and Dan got a glimpse of the woman his dad had been captivated by this past year. The first thing that caught his attention was her easy smile and attractive, yet not glamorous look. She wore black leggings and a comfortable long cream loose fitting tee with an animal print scarf tied at her neck, and canvas loafers. Diane had the appearance of a woman who prized comfort over any need to garner attention. Her shoulder length prematurely gray hair was tied up in a loose knot on top of her head, and she looked to be about Harold's age.

Dan scurried around to the curb side of the car and went to grab her travel bag as he reached out his hand to greet her at the same time. She presented a warm side, eagerly drawing him in for a quick hug instead of taking his outstretched hand. "I'm so happy to finally meet you," she told him. Dan tried to disguise his shock at her warmth, such a contrast to his father.

Right behind her, his dad smiled broadly at his son and also came in for an embrace. That was unexpected as could be, and Dan felt wary, but also hopeful that this lovely woman might have somehow brought out a side of Harold that he had never seen.

Harold suggested that Diane sit in the front seat so that Dan could point out the local points of interest as they made their way through Charlotte and home to Beacon. She proved to be an interesting companion and the two easily conversed on the hour drive back home. Dan took the opportunity to ask her how she met his dad.

"Oh," she said, "it was not love at first sight, not by any means. I catered lunches in the building where he works and when I first met your dad he was anything but friendly. As a matter of fact, after a couple of weeks I called him out about his rudeness."

Dan wasn't the least bit surprised to hear that. He wondered how his dad felt about her sharing. Glancing in the rearview mirror, he saw that his dad had covered his ears with headphones and wasn't paying any attention to their conversation. He told her, "Well, that must have changed at some point. How did he take it when you called him out?"

She told Dan, "I think it shocked him. I think he was used to people just accepting the behavior from him. It was the funniest thing. He actually seemed curious about what I meant by it. Asked me out for a drink after work later that week. I almost declined, but there was such sadness in him. I wanted to get to know him and I guess I was a bit intrigued."

She changed the subject once they started driving through Beacon, "Harold has told me so much about this quaint little town, and it sure doesn't disappoint," she remarked looking this way, then that, to catch everything she could. Dan had to bite his tongue to keep from expressing his surprise at her comments about his father chatting it up with her about the town that hadn't seemed special to his dad at all.

Once home, and entering through the large oak door, Diane told Harold and Dan what a beautiful home they had. "Is Stacy here?" she asked Dan.

"She's over at the B&B welcoming those who are staying there for the wedding weekend. She's working long hours for us right now."

Dan's dad inquired, "Did I hear you say in the car on the way here that she is dating Norm Meade?" Dan nodded affirmatively and said he thought that was probably the biggest incentive for her staying put.

"I was glad to hear that. Your mom and I used to enjoy Norm and Barb's company when you were a little guy. He's a good man." Turning to Diane he told her that Norm had lost Barb a couple of years ago, then said they should make plans after the wedding to go out for dinner with Norm and Stacy.

Dan had the oddest sensation that this was his dad, but also wasn't. What had happened? Had they entered the twilight zone? Now Harold was showing interest in an old neighbor, on top of stated plans to stay beyond the wedding. He told Diane and his dad, "I know Stacy is getting her things together to stay at the B&B while you're here. She may not have had time to gather everything yet. I'm afraid we have her working around the clock."

"Nonsense," Harold remarked. "She doesn't have to move out of the guest room on our account. This place is big enough for the three of us, and you'll be able to host more guests that way." Dan was so taken aback by his dad's kind and thoughtful words that all he could do was nod. All he could conjure was that Diane must have worked wonders in him over the past few months.

Just then Stacy burst through the front door, eager to meet the man who had allowed her to live in his home while he was away in London, and equally excited about meeting Diane.

Dan made the introductions then asked Stacy, "How are things going over at the inn? You must be exhausted, but Dad has good news for you. He and Diane want you to stay on in the house while they are here for our wedding. You can at least take moving temporarily to the B&B off your plate."

"Oh my goodness that's incredible!" Stacy exclaimed. "Are you absolutely sure you don't mind my being here?"

Diane quickly answered her question, smiling and placing a welcoming hand on Stacy's wrist, "Absolutely sure. We can't wait to get to know you. Dan told us that you are dating an old friend of Harold's. Any old friend of Harold's is someone I am eager to get to know as well."

Stacy drew Diane into a quick hug. "I'm happy you are here, and thanks for letting me stay. Takes so much off my plate. Would you two like a tour of the inn?" She winked at Dan, "I guess you are the one to show them around."

Dan told Stacy to stay home for dinner and put her feet up before going back to work. "I'm going over to get Kate anyway. I'll give them the tour," he assured her.

Chapter 26

AS KATE AND DAN WALKED OVER to what had been her home for the past five years for dinner with Brooks and Reese, Dan filled her in on meeting Diane and the drive home. "Pinch me."

"Ouch," he chuckled, "Not literally!" Jabbing her gently in her side, he wrapped her up in an embrace on her old front porch. He could hardly believe that in two days they would be married at last.

"C'mon in," Brooks welcomed them. "Just be careful not to trip over any boxes."

"This feels strange, but also somehow right," Kate said. "Is Reese in the kitchen?"

"I think she's throwing a salad together."

Kate said, "I hope that's all she's doing. I can't believe you can even find your dishes. You just moved in!"

"Oh, my wife is an organizer extraordinaire; she has the kitchen ready to go. She said she's so happy to have a kitchen—not because of living at your place, but having lost ours after the storm."

Reese came in and joined the conversation. "I made a chicken casserole that my friend Suzanne gave me a few years ago and told me whenever I had fifteen minutes to get something in the oven, that could be my go-to." She told them it bakes for two hours and would be ready in half an hour, then set down the chilled Sauvignon Blanc on a sturdy cardboard box/coffee table and poured them each a glass.

"You didn't bring yourself a glass. I'll go grab one for you," Dan offered.

"No, thanks, Dan. I'm not having any tonight." She subconsciously drew her hands protectively over her flat stomach.

Kate picked up on the gesture, "Reese, are you—"

Reese shot a glance over to Brooks who nodded his head as if to say, okay, go ahead...

"Yes! We are expecting. We just found out and we weren't going to tell—"

Kate wrapped her up in a happy hug before she could finish her sentence. "Oh my gosh, that is the best, most exciting news!"

Dan drew Brooks in for a bear hug, "Wow, man, great news. Congratulations!"

Reese shyly shared, "We weren't going to tell anyone just yet so if we could keep it between us for a couple of months—"

"Of course," Kate assured her. "Best secret ever!"

"I just hope morning sickness stays away long enough for me to feel good walking down the aisle as a bridesmaid. I sure don't want to throw up on anyone!" She giggled. "Oh, that was gross. Let's go eat now that I've mentioned my biggest, everyone-will-want-to eat-right-after-I've-said-that fear."

On their walk home Kate and Dan talked about the evening, their excitement about their friends' news, and how good that chicken dish had been. "I'm going to ask Reese if I can put that on the fall menu. A recipe that's quick to put together and tastes that good, I hope she agrees."

"Enough shop talk," Kate turned to him as they were getting in the car so he could drop her off at her mom's and Jack's house for the next two nights. "I'd rather put that mouth of yours to better use." He had to agree that the kiss was a far better idea.

"Let's just sit in this car and practice. We want it to be perfected by Saturday," he teased her.

"Mmhm," was all she managed as she tilted her face up to his.

*   *   *

Suzanne's chicken casserole

- 8 boned chicken breasts

- 1 c raw rice

- 1 T melted butter

- 1 can cream of mushroom soup

- 1 can cream of celery soup

- 1 can cream of chicken soup

- 2 T white wine vinegar

- Grated cheddar

- Sliced almonds

Bone chicken breasts and set aside

Melt butter, put in casserole dish and stir in rice.

Pour ½ can of each of the soups over rice.

Place chicken on top of rice.

Mix remaining soup and vinegar. Top chicken with this.

Sprinkle with grated cheese and almonds.

Bake at 350 for 1 and ½ hours covered, then for ½ hour uncovered.

Chapter 27

THE NEXT MORNING KATE WOKE UP AT JACK and Maggie's country house when the sun peeked its way into her guest room window. The day promised to be beautiful, as did their wedding day as well, and she felt grateful since almost every single thing they had planned was going to be held outside. Her mom poked her head in to make sure she was up. Kate was hosting the bridesmaids at a brunch over at Mary's Restaurant on the covered back patio later in the morning.

"How are you?" Maggie sat down next to her on the bed to check in with her daughter. She put her hands on Kate's shoulders, faced her, "Two very big days in your beautiful life."

"I'm just lying here thinking about how happy I am, how long I have waited and finally, it's here! You are right about that. My life is beautiful, and I'm guessing you feel the same way about yours." Gazing into her mom's eyes, she saw true contentment and peace that hadn't always been there. "Sometimes all I want is for nothing to change. For things to stay just like they are. Forever. These next two days are going to fly by. I just know it, but I am truly so grateful and happy with my life."

"Just be present, every single moment," her mom advised, "and treasure this time."

Kate and Maggie were at the restaurant by 10:45 so she could place the bridesmaid gifts at each place setting. Before Ali, Jenny, Shanti, Amy, and Reese arrived, she ordered pitchers of mimosas and fresh strawberry scones with fruit plates for appetizers. Mary usually only provided brunch on Sunday, and Kate was overjoyed that she was offering it to them on a Friday. It was her favorite, and she knew everyone would enjoy the food as they sat under the shade of the historic water tower.

Kate felt pretty dressed in her white sundress and wedge sandals; she hardly ever dressed up. At her neck rested the classic pearl necklace Maggie had given her as a wedding gift, providing the "something old" as it had been passed down from Maggie's mom, to Maggie, and now to Kate.

Maggie looked beautiful as well in the dress she had worn just weeks before at her courthouse wedding. She was so relieved that Kate had accepted her apologies and that things were good between them again.

As the rest of the party arrived, Kate and Maggie offered them scones and mimosas, laughing at the festive way they were indulging on a weekday morning. Kate made sure to covertly offer Reese a virgin mimosa and told her to be sure that she always took hers from Kate. She winked conspiratorially as she referenced the happy secret.

"Everyone, please take your seats," Kate smiled as her eyes passed over the women she loved most in her life. "There's a gift waiting for you to open. I'm beyond honored to have each of you walk down the aisle ahead of me. I love you all so much. I can't remember a time when I didn't."

Maggie took her seat and exclaimed, "You didn't need to get anything for me. I'm not a bridesmaid."

"You've got to be kidding, Mom. I wouldn't think of leaving you out. Open them already, everyone!"

They quickly obeyed, and oohed and ahhed over the stunning blue topaz necklaces they would all be wearing with their champagne hued dresses. Each woman had selected her own, and the styles they chose flattered their figures. The mostly blue hydrangea bouquets would complete their look. Kate thought they would be dressed beautifully for an outdoor summer wedding, and like all brides, she hoped her bridesmaids could wear the dresses again.

SIX O'CLOCK SHARP THEY RAN THROUGH the wedding rehearsal at the B&B, then went out to the country. Their main objective was for all invited to have fun and enjoy Friday night and Saturday as much as they did. Jack and Maggie had done their part, hiring three Charlotte area food trucks to park beside the driveway flanking the pond. Everyone was encouraged to dress comfortably and casually.

Tables and chairs were set up under the oaks and pines surrounding the pond. They had hired Tammy to create informal tablescapes and asked her to use as much as she could from their acreage. She strung lights on the tree branches. Basically, she created the same magic that she had for the Christmas Eve festivities the night Dan and Kate had shared their first kiss, the first after ten years apart anyway, and officially became a couple.

The bar was set up next to the food trucks and guests could select from an assortment of wine and beer. It had been hard to narrow down the food trucks to three, but they had landed on Carolina barbecue, Mexican, and the best dessert truck in the land.

Friends of Kate's and Maggie's from way back, Danika and The Jeb were setting up to perform the background music for the night and also would be singing at the wedding. They had begun performing about fifteen years ago, moved to Nashville and sang at home concerts and small venues all around the country. They had been given the best suite in the B&B, a small way to thank them for giving them two nights of entertainment. Their acoustic, pop, soul sound was absolutely magical.

Before sitting down to feast, Dan and Kate, hand in hand, floated rather than strolled, from table to table, making sure they greeted everyone. If anyone had asked them to describe their joy, they wouldn't have found the words. No one needed to though. All one had to do was look at the two of them.

They sat down at a table with Maggie and Jack, Ali and Justin, and Harold and Diane. Normally, Dan would have felt uneasy with his dad there, but after the uncanny afternoon yesterday he felt strangely at peace. And as conversation flowed easily around the table, it felt to Dan and Kate like the perfect wedding gift.

Chapter 28

JUNE 9TH ARRIVED AND WITH IT the festivities began as Kate and Maggie co-taught a yoga class to those willing to rise early and laugh their way through it.

Kate scanned the packed yoga room and saw those who regularly practiced... Tammy, Eunice, Emma, Dale, Charlie, Sam, Marie, Norm, Stacy, Kim, Dee, Jenny, Chris, Shanti, Jack and Mimi. She noticed those who never practiced or even thought of stepping foot on a yoga mat... David, Joyce, Harold, Jon. So much love in the room!

They put on a wedding song playlist, laughed, fell over, practiced, giggled, took things seriously for a moment, chuckled...

If there was a better way to begin the day, she didn't know what it was. Well, maybe that Dan could have been there, but there were some wedding traditions worth keeping. He wouldn't see her until she walked down the aisle.

An hour later Dan was talking with his dad. "Dan, there are some things I want to tell you, and I'm wondering if you would mind walking over to your mom's gravesite with me so she can be a part of it?"

"Uh, sure, I guess," Dan replied.

Father and son set off to walk over to an important place that they had never walked over to together before. They sat down on the ground near her marker, and brushed off the bit of debris that had blown onto it. Gazing up at the heavens, Harold wiped a tear from the corner of his eye. Dan had never seen that before. "June, can you believe our son is getting married today? It seems like yesterday when I was over the moon in love with you, Junebug. You were an amazing mother, wife, and best friend. I threw myself way too much into work and way too little into our lives together. I will regret that for the rest of my life, honey, and I am so very sorry."

He went on to tell his son, "I never took the time to feel, to sit and grieve. I just plunged into work, and it became my end all, my be all. It never made me happy. It just became a hamster wheel that kept rolling on. I was a man obsessed with work. I was a jerk. Worse."

He looked at Dan, allowing the tears to fall. "It took getting to know Diane, opening up to the possibility of love, being willing to let her help me see, and change…please forgive me. I know I don't deserve it, but if you could see your way to giving me another chance… I just wonder if you ever could."

Dan was quiet for a few minutes, still digesting everything his dad just said to him and to his mom. "Dad, I love you and I want to forgive you. And I want this day to be the start of something new. We can go forward and try for it to be different between us." Dan couldn't completely forgive him right then. He thought his dad's remorse was genuine, but there was so much harm that had been done over the years. He'd wanted it to be different so many times, and he hoped it could be in the future. But the scars were deep.

"His dad managed a smile. He hesitated, then asked his son. "Would you be okay with me moving back? Diane and I want to live here, at least for a while."

"I think that's a good start, Dad. We can take it slowly and just see what happens."

BACK AT THE B&B Stacy had reserved the upstairs room and spacious new bath for the bride and her bridesmaids to prepare. Once Kate was dressed in her gown, she turned to face her attendants. She looked absolutely stunning in her a-line princess off the shoulder white chiffon dress with lace beaded flowers covering the bodice. She wore her hair in soft waves covered in a pearl and crystal bridal hair vine that trailed softly through the waves. Her makeup was soft with the only nod to glamorous being false eyelashes that made her hazel eyes pop.

It was a good thing that the bridesmaids and her mom hadn't put on their makeup yet. Most of them had tears in their eyes. It wasn't just the look, it was the happiness that shone through her smile, her countenance.

OVER AT THE CAFE, the men were relaxed, not overdoing it by any means, but enjoying one beer each and gobbling up the meal Dan made of burgers, cole slaw, and homemade french fries.

What more could a guy want?

The most spectacular thing of all was seeing his dad interact with Justin, Brooks, Chris, Joe, and Andy. They were seeing a new side of Harold and were not outwardly acting the least surprised. Dan presented each of them with personalized glass beer mugs and classic tie bars to wear with their khaki linen suits at the wedding. Blue neckties the color of hydrangeas completed their ensembles.

They sat around eating, and ribbing Dan about his love for Kate and basically telling stories from the past. Dan noticed that Jack and Harold were hitting it off and that made him happy.

A LOW COUNTRY BOIL WAS BEING PREPARED in the farthest reaches of the yard to be served at the reception after the wedding ceremony. There

were three forty gallon pots. Red potatoes, corn, onions, crab boil seasoning, lemons, sausage, and seafood were stacked everywhere. The smell was
going to entice everyone from a couple of miles around, it seemed.

Chapter 29

AND IT WAS TIME. Friends and family were seated facing the gazebo, which was covered in roses, hydrangeas, jasmine, and gardenias. They watched the bridesmaids proceed down the soft grassy center aisle, and stand to celebrate Maggie walking her lovely daughter to a beaming Dan, flanked by his groomsmen. The simple ceremony brought tears to almost everyone's eyes. There wasn't a guest present who wondered for a second if this pair wasn't a match made in heaven. And no one was happier than the bride and groom. Dan couldn't take his eyes off his gorgeous bride, the woman he would finally be with forever.

Guests and the wedding party circulated afterwards on the beautiful grounds that had been cleared and manicured to perfection. Clearly, this B&B would become a destination wedding site in the future. But no one was thinking about that today. Champagne was flowing, revelers were reveling, and the late afternoon celebration was continuing into the evening.

Jack and Maggie found a moment to themselves and he finally had a chance to tell her the news that he felt confident she would love. They were alone at a table under the reception tent. "Mags," he took her hand, "I have a surprise for you, and I'm thinking unlike the last one, you're going to like this one."

"Oh oh," she giggled and took a sip of champagne. "I hope so."

"Ali helped me plan a honeymoon for the two of us and we are leaving tomorrow as soon as you get packed."

"So when is the flight and where are we going? Will I have time to pack and not be rushed?"

"We will be driving so you can take your sweet time," he said. "Ali and Justin offered us their beach house. She thought you'd love it."

Maggie threw her arms around his neck and squealed, "Perfect. Just perfect! Oh my goodness, is Kate okay with my being gone, um, there's the studio to consider, and—"

"Honey," he kissed her. "Every detail has been worked out."

"In that case, I'm thinking I might start liking your surprises after all." She kissed him back.

Joe and Shanti were sitting down alone enjoying a glass of wine. Joe started teasing her a little about noticing she was tearing up during the wedding ceremony. "What was going on? You looked like you were going to cry during their vows."

"I was!" Shanti took his hands in hers. "I just felt so inspired by their love. And Joe, I know it has been hard for you, your first marriage ending like it did. But I want you to know something. I love you, and you can count on that."

He looked at her as he put down his wine glass. "You love me? You do? Oh, Shanti, I am in love with you too." He kissed her with such tenderness.

TIME FOR DINNER. The reception tent had been set up behind the house and was filled with rustic touches, just right for the low country boil dinner everyone would be enjoying. The wedding party was introduced and each couple danced in to fun choreographed moves, followed by the happily married Dan and Kate.

They danced afterwards to their favorite love song, and slowly the dance floor filled with friends and family. Perfection.

Later, much later, as Stacy and Norm walked back to Harold's house, Norm paused on the way when they reached his. Under a canopy of stars, he stopped walking on the sidewalk in front of his home, the very place they had first met on the way to the yin class. Moonlight lit their faces and he took her in his arms. "Stacy, this is the spot where we first met, remember?"

"Of course," she murmured.

They walked on to Harold's. He looked over at her as they quietly went on their way, Norm wondered what she was thinking.

What she was thinking was, 'I hope we can keep this'.

BACK AT THE B&B Dan and Kate found themselves alone in the gazebo enjoying a piece of their wedding cake. Other than the bites they had stuffed into each other's mouths for the photo earlier, they hadn't taken the time to enjoy it. Kate looked into her husband's eyes, "Isn't life wonderful, the way one day I was just leaving my studio, and there you were? I can still hardly believe it."

"Believe it, love, because not only was I there that day, but you are stuck with me for the rest of your life." He lifted his left hand to point out his wedding band. She placed her left hand over his.

Kate grinned. "Let's get in that wonderful old house and start the rest of our lives right now."

Acknowledgements

To my amazing daughters, Ali Georgacakis and Kate Kole who painstakingly read and reread. Their encouragement kept me on task.

To my loving husband Jack who listened as I read one or two or three chapters a day. (This is not his genre).

To my dear friends Robin Olson and Donna Ramsey whose editing was invaluable.

To those who let me use their first names.

And to you, who chose to read this novel…

My gratitude.

About the author...

Terry is mother to three, grandmother to six, and wife of almost 46 years to Jack. Having lived all over the country, she and Jack recently settled down in the quaint town of Waxhaw, North Carolina, where she found the inspiration and time to write her first novel, Second Chance at Christmastime, and this novel, the second in the Beacon Series.

She is an avid reader, yoga teacher, and loves good food.